# Coming Attractions

Mark R. Hunter

Other titles by Mark R. Hunter

Non-fiction:
Images of America: Albion and Noble County
Smoky Days and Sleepless Nights: A Century or So With the
Albion Fire Department
Slightly Off the Mark
Hoosier Hysterical: How the West Became the Midwest
Without Moving At All

Fiction:
Storm Chaser
Storm Chaser Shorts
The Notorious Ian Grant
The No-Campfire Girls
Radio Red

Edited by Emily Hunter
Cover by Emily Hunter

ISBN-13: 978-1729748121
ISBN-10: 1729748120

For book extras and additional books by the author, please visit: www.MarkRHunter.com

*In loving memory of*
*Linda Taylor*
*Jean Coonts Stroud*

Special thanks to the Auburn-Garrett Drive-In;

The drive-in movie theaters still upholding the tradition;

And all the drive-ins of our youth: especially, for me, the High-Vue of Kendallville, Indiana

# Coming Attractions

Mark R. Hunter

# CHAPTER ONE

Maddie saw trouble ahead as soon as she stepped off the company airplane.

The kid standing in the terminal held a slab of cardboard before him like a shield, with her name plastered in red across its surface. Maybe he was attempting to hide the fact that, beneath the wrinkled black suit coat, he wore a white T-shirt that should have been washed at least two meals ago. More likely he feared missing her, since a quick study of the shaggy haired young man told her he held little stock in appearances.

"Madison McKinley?" He gave her an equally appraising scan.

Stopping before him, she deliberately looked right and left. The closest other people stood at least two hundred feet away, gathered around the airport's gift shop. "Maddie."

Taking that as encouragement, he smiled. "Tupper. Welcome to Fort Wayne!" He still held the sign up.

"Tupper?"

"That's my name—well, my middle name, and that's what I go by. My mother sold Tupperware, and she's pretty hardcore. I don't know if they still hold Tupperware parties, but if you want her to set one up—"

"I doubt I'll be here that long." Maddie tried not to judge people by appearances, but Tupper looked for all the world like Shaggy from the Scooby Doo cartoon series—without the goatee. Under other circumstances she might have been tempted to smile. "Tupper, were you expecting a company plane?"

"Oh, sure. I've been with the company over a week now."

"And did anyone get off the plane besides me?"

His brow knitted in concentration. "Nope."

"Then do you really believe the sign is necessary?"

Face reddening, Tupper dropped the cardboard. "Sorry."

"Trash can, Tupper—let's keep our planet clean." She blushed a little, herself—it wasn't fair to take her mood out on him.

When Tupper turned to throw the sign away, Maddie realized he wore a fairly nice pair of navy slacks—and white sneakers. "Are you, by chance, related to one of the partners?"

"I'm Mr. Quincy's great-nephew—how did you know?"

"Family resemblance." Maddie despised lying, but saw no reason to hurt someone's feelings. Nepotism could be a powerful force—why else would this kid be hired by the stuffiest law firm in Boston? "You were to bring a car?"

"This way." Tupper turned, paused, then whirled around. "Did you have luggage?"

"I'm a woman, Tupper." This time she did smile.

He frowned.

"That means yes. Two bags."

After retrieving her luggage, Tupper led the way into the warmth of a sunny June midafternoon. "You'll love Fort Wayne. They have an orchestra, a zoo, a mall, three rivers ..." He trailed off, thinking.

"It seemed a bit small from the air." *The poor guy might hurt himself if his brain doesn't cool down.*

"Well, it's the second largest city in Indiana."

As they walked across the crowded parking lot a breeze swirled the folds of Maddie's skirt and blew blonde strands of hair across her face. "Large by Indiana standards? Not a telling argument."

"But you come from Boston. Indiana's a lot bigger than Massachusetts."

"In square miles, maybe," Maddie murmured under her breath. She almost ran into Tupper when he skidded to a halt. "Where's the car?"

"Right here." He pointed to a deep purple Chrysler van.

She stared, trying to fend off a wave of nostalgia for her Porsche. "I asked for a sedan."

"Yeah, you traded up—isn't that great?" He produced a key ring from his pocket and pushed the unlock button. "It's got a digital audio system, sliding doors on both sides, an environmental readout, and you gotta love the color. It's a real love machine."

Such a statement could only come from a member of the Scooby Gang. Maddie stared at him, hands on hips, but held her temper—after all, her temper got her here to begin with. "I realize you've been by yourself here, but since you arrived with just two jobs—to get me a hotel room and a car—could it be that difficult?"

"I didn't actually arrive—I grew up west of here, in New Haven." He noticed her expression, and stumbled backward. "Um, there's a car show at the Memorial Coliseum—by the way, we have a Memorial Coliseum—and Jay Leno's going to be there and all the rental cars were taken and this is the only—"

"Tupper, Calm down." Maddie took him by the shoulder, which made the younger man flinch. "Maybe this is for the best. Don't people going to drive-in movies often take vans?"

He blinked at her. "Yeah, sure. I like to back my truck in, when I'm not working. Why?"

Oh, dear—He didn't know why she'd been sent. "Because I've never visited one, and I might have some free time while I'm here."

Tupper brightened instantly. "The best one in Indiana is about an hour north of Fort Wayne—you'll love it."

She very much doubted that. "Tupper, do you know why I'm here?"

"Um—" He paused, trying to focus. "To expand the agency's influence into business dealings in the Midwest."

"Which means?"

"Got me." He shrugged. "This is my first assignment since I visited Uncle Quincy, but he said it was real important, so I figure I'm on the fast track."

Uncle Quincy? What an image—like Luciano Pavarotti breakdancing. "You are, indeed." Maddie decided she liked the kid, after all. She couldn't help thinking of him as a kid, although he couldn't be more than five years younger than her, and he seemed sincere in his desire to help. Besides, in his own way he was exiled here, just like her. "Do you have transportation?"

"My truck—oh, you mean here?" He gestured to a yellow Volkswagen Beetle parked beside the van. Inside, a girl with spiked

4

green hair waved, then went back to studying her eyebrow ring in the rear view mirror. *How entirely appropriate.*

"Tupper, you've obviously been working hard. Why don't you take a day or two off? Visit with your family, take a short break, and contact me at the hotel later."

"Really? Wow, thanks! I needed to take off for my part time job soon, anyway." He started to hop into the Beetle, but paused when she called his name.

"It might be helpful to have the information packet your great-uncle promised me. Not to mention the van keys."

"Oh!" Tupper handed her the keys and gestured toward the van. "There's a folder on the passenger seat with maps, directions, your reservation, and a really big book about John Adams. He's my ancestor, you know. I think he was governor, or something."

"Possibly the genes have thinned out since then." Ignoring his puzzled expression, she climbed into the van.

"Well, if you like to go to the drive-in you'll probably see me there. Take it easy!" The Bug roared away.

After a moment Maddie got back out, opened the rear door, and threw in the luggage Tupper had abandoned on the pavement. Sincere he may be, competent he may not.

Maddie spent some time reading the directions and comparing them to the maps. Smiling despite herself, she also leafed through the biography of John Adams. Inside the front cover she found a short inscription: "John Adams called himself obnoxious and unpopular— but he got the job done. Quincy."

Adam Quincy had been named for the second President, and according to rumor was a distant relative. Maddie considered John Adams a role model for his courage and perseverance, but that, and

5

their occupation, was all she and Quincy had in common. Leave it to the law firm's founder to turn a gift into a subtle reminder of who was in charge.

She spotted some brochures in the folder. Tupper apparently thought her job involved sightseeing: He'd enclosed something about every tourist destination in northeast Indiana, from zoos and state parks to an Old Jail Museum. And a drive-in movie theater.

The colorful advertisement declared this to be the 50th anniversary of the High View Drive-In. Two features for the whole family every night, all summer long, plus weekend showings in the spring and fall. Photos showed happy families who munched on popcorn and other snacks while watching the latest flick from the comfort of their automobiles.

Maddie studied every detail, every letter, and then determined the hotel would not, after all, be her next destination. It was getting close to dusk. She had a van, and other than being a bit overdressed for the movies she should go unnoticed.

Yes, a visit to the drive-in was clearly in order. After all, she well remembered one of the first rules from law school: Know your enemy.

Despite her black mood on the airplane, the weather and the masses of greenery Maddie passed during her drive north cheered her a bit. She'd believed as a child that a field was a dirt lot for baseball, and the biggest patch of plant life no more than a Boston city park. Her preteen mind couldn't have imagined these expanses of woods, or unlimited stretches of young corn and wheat.

It was cool enough to shut down the air conditioner and crack the windows, an act that would horrify her hairstylist. Considering the obscene amounts of money she paid the man, by now he should have come up with a wave that would last through a tornado.

She missed him. She missed her Porsche mechanic, her personal assistant, the doorman, and all the partners with their custom tailored suits, ten dollar cigars, and condescending attitudes. No matter how important this assignment, everyone knew it was punishment. She must prove herself all over again if she ever expected a corner office and her pick of cases.

A few miles after turning onto a two lane highway she spotted the sign, a gaudy red and yellow monstrosity guaranteed to attract attention. The top formed an arrow pointing toward the metal framework of the movie screen, and below the arrow stood a sign advertising a Pixar animated movie and a teen comedy.

To Maddie's surprise half a dozen cars already lined the drive. A van similar to hers waited first behind the closed gate to the ticket booth, with the adult occupants of the other vehicles gathered around it. They looked like they were having a conference, or maybe a tailgate party. A dozen young people, from teens to toddlers, played in a grassy area between the drive and a red fence that surrounded the property.

Maddie stopped behind the last vehicle, wincing at the crunch of gravel beneath her wheels. Clearly, Indiana needed to invest in more asphalt. After the dust cleared, she opened her windows all the way to admit the scent of freshly mowed grass and a far off barbecue, then shut off the engine. Country music played from the pickup in front of her, but it was the sound of kids screaming that made her stiffen.

She scanned around the lawn until certain they were screams of glee, not pain. Why didn't these parents pay closer attention to their children? Wouldn't it be safer to keep them in their cars, instead of wandering around where they could get hit, or fall, or be bitten by snakes or rabid bunnies or something? Not to mention all the strangers.

Well, she must be the only stranger here, considering everyone else still gathered around the one vehicle. The scene would make someone nostalgic, if that someone held memories of going to the movies. Maddie remembered only a few trips to a more traditional theater.

She'd been led to believe little local support remained for the drive-in, making a buyout easy. Except for one lonely old house along the drive-in property, the surrounding land consisted of farm fields and small tracts of woods, most optioned by the development company her firm represented.

The drive-in's owner remained the holdout, and by bad luck his property made up the bull's-eye in the tract of land the developer needed. The better his business, the harder her job—and here people already waited, on a weeknight, no less.

Perhaps this made up the hardcore locals with nothing better to do. You couldn't make profit margin with six customers a day.

That optimistic thought faded when an old station wagon pulled up behind her van, pumping rock and roll into the air, as a full house gyrated inside.

With a sigh, Maddie examined the customers. Their dress consisted of shorts or blue jeans, and tank tops or printed tees. She glanced down at her silk print dress, and determined not to leave the van under any circumstances. The average person might not know the difference between her expensive outfit and something from an outlet store, but she would still stand out.

Soon adults began to saunter back toward their own vehicles, while the kids ran, jumping and shouting, to join them. She held her breath until she was sure none of the children would trip or get hit by a car door, then turned to see a woman move the gate aside and climb into the ticket booth. Maddie switched the engine on and wondered if kid movies had changed much since "The Little Mermaid".

Soon Maddie caught sight of the ticket price, painted on the

8

whitewashed side of the ticket booth, and took a sharp breath. It was a third of what she'd expect to pay in downtown Boston. How in the world could this man stay in business, with prices so low? The popcorn must be a dollar a kernel.

The ticket taker held an animated conversation with everyone in line, but managed to keep customers moving until Maddie stopped before her. Then the woman, who wore a white T-shirt proclaiming "The High View—50 years and counting," did a double take and leaned in for a closer look.

"You're a little overdressed for the movies, ain't ya, hon?"

"The philharmonic was sold out." Maddie gritted her teeth, although she'd expected this reaction.

Now the woman leaned closer, to take in the clean, empty interior of the van. "Just you?"

"Is that all right?"

The woman arched an eyebrow. "Okay by me, just kinda unusual. Why go see a movie by yourself?"

"My boyfriend plays in the philharmonic."

"Well ..." With a shake of her head, the woman handed Maddie a ticket stub, then rattled off an FM radio frequency. "Enjoy the show. Oh! I almost forgot." She gave Maddie a bumper sticker.

Beneath a red, white and blue drawing of the movie screen, colorful letters spelled out: "Save the High View! Half a Century and Counting."

The woman leaned forward and hissed, "Some big company out east wants to turn it into an airport!"

"Oh, my."

"Don't worry, we'll fight 'em and win. You have a good time now, hon."

"Thank you," Maddie answered automatically. As she drove through the lot, she saw similar stickers on all the parked vehicles. The other van, she noted, differed from hers in only two ways: It was black instead of deep purple, and sported stickers on the back and side windows. As she passed it she saw a pair of bright hazel eyes regard her curiously through the rear view mirror, and wondered whether it was because of the twin transportation, or because she drove the only auto in the lot without a show of support pasted on every surface.

*Where to park?* In the middle of the lot sat a low concrete block structure painted white, with two doors on each side: one for a restroom and another for an entrance to the snack area. Maddie had no intention of abandoning her nutrition plan. Still, she could imagine a need for the restroom if, for some reason, she decided to stay through both movies.

Of course she would stay. She needed to know as much as possible about this business, in order to get it shut down. The best place for her would be at the corner closest to the women's restroom, but, ironically, the other purple van had already staked it out. Maddie settled for a spot at the other front corner.

All the old concrete speaker posts stood empty. Didn't the ticket taker say something about a radio frequency? Dialing it in produced a crooning Norah Jones, but Maddie assumed she had the right place, left it on, and began watching the incoming traffic.

She made some quick calculations, based on the ticket price, the average number of people per car, and the cost of electricity, payroll, and other overhead. She factored in snacks, then cut food profit in half when she noticed many of the moviegoers brought their own. Despite that, by the time the sun disappeared behind a low, distant cloud bank, the place had already broken even. When the first preview for upcoming movies appeared, it was turning a profit.

On a *weeknight*. Not good at all.

Maddie sat back, paying little attention to the ads. She leaned forward again when a group of teens walked by, loaded down with nachos, popcorn, and soda. Her stomach began a low, rumbling litany of complaints. When did she last eat? Not dinner. Not lunch, come to think of it, except for a bag of peanuts on the plane.

So much for staying in the car. So much for her diet, unless the snack bar featured something no one she saw had purchased. But it was now too dark for anyone to notice her style of dress, and this could be the perfect opportunity to investigate the operation further. After all, she was here on a job, and if she wanted to erase her black marks with the company she needed to perform it well.

That determination lasted until she reached the door to the snack bar, and realized her miscalculation. Of course it was too dark to see her dress, and the expensive style of her blonde tresses, and the opal necklace and charm bracelet—outside. Inside, fluorescent light made it bright as day.

But with the movie starting, nobody stood before the long counter with its popcorn machine, soda fountain, and snack rack. At least, nobody until she came in one way while, at the same moment, a man burst through the opposite door.

They both froze, regarding each other. She recognized the twinkling hazel eyes and the sandy, disheveled hair at once, although he looked taller when out from behind the wheel. He wore jeans and a white T-shirt with the all too familiar drive-in logo on it, along with the words "Drive-Ins are for Cars, not Planes". Admirably muscled arms clutched an empty popcorn bucket.

The man smiled, flashing teeth so perfect it brought back memories of the thousands of dollars Maddie sunk into her orthodonture, and walked toward her. Of their own volition Maddie's legs also moved, until they met in front of the cash register.

"Are you lost?" His baritone voice sent a jolt up her spine, and suddenly exile in Indiana didn't seem so bad.

"I'm ... um ..." She glanced around to remind herself where she was. "I'm looking for healthy food."

"You *are* lost." He smiled again. "I meant you don't look like the drive-in type."

If you're the drive-in type, Maddie thought, get me a season ticket. "It was spur of the moment." True enough.

"I've been there." He held a hand out. "Logan. Logan Chandler."

She felt her hand enveloped in his warmth. His touch, firm but gentle, made her catch her breath. She tried to stutter out her name, and found she couldn't remember.

"Maddie!" someone else called.

The idea of anyone in Indiana knowing her came as such a shock that Maddie pulled her hand away and turned, almost backing into the wall. Behind the counter, swathed in an apron that didn't completely cover the drive-in emblem on his white T-shirt, a wild haired young man grinned at her.

"Tupper?"

"I told you we'd meet again if you came to the drive-in. This is my part time job."

Uh oh. Maddie glanced at Logan, who turned from her to Tupper with a raised eyebrow. While Tupper didn't know everything about her mission, it would be easy to put two and two together.

"I guess I assumed you're not from around here at all," Logan said,

12

eyeing her dress.

"Tupper and I just met today." Good, the truth. But Maddie couldn't grasp where to go from there. "It's a long story, and the movie's started."

"But you know each other?"

"Absolutely." Again, true enough.

Tupper pitched in, "We're like old friends, dude."

"Okay." Smiling again, Logan grandly gestured Maddie forward. "I just need to replace some spilled popcorn. After you."

What? Oh. She turned to Tupper, determined to get out of there before he gave her away. Logan might be a lost Greek god, but she couldn't afford to get involved with him, especially after the last fiasco in her love life. "Perrier?"

"Huh?" Tupper stared at her, open mouthed. "I don't know Spanish."

Behind her, Logan chuckled, making her even more aware of his presence.

"Do you serve any bottled water?" In truth, Maddie craved some decent coffee, but she had a feeling her definition of "decent" wouldn't fit here.

"Oh!" Tupper grabbed a bottle of water with a brand name she didn't recognize. "This is local. It comes out of a spring well right by a church."

"And a cemetery," Logan offered. She looked back to find him grinning wickedly. "Imagine that."

She did, but took the bottle anyway. "Is there anything to eat that doesn't involve large amounts of sugar or carbohydrates?"

"Uh—" Tupper glanced around wildly. "No."

"Get her some of the world famous popcorn, Tupper," Logan said. "On me."

"Popcorn on you." For some reason Tupper found that amusing, and chuckled as he scooped the white kernels up.

"No salt or butter, please." Maddie felt a touch on her arm, and turned to see Logan smiling yet again.

"No salt or butter? That's cardboard."

Could she make herself look any more out of place? "I'm twenty-nine years old." When he gave her a questioning look, she added, "I can't eat whatever I want, not anymore." As if she ever could.

He raked his gaze over Maddie, making her gulp and shiver. "You don't have an ounce of fat on you."

That was a compliment, she assumed. Maddie didn't have an ounce of fat, not even on her chest—or at least, that had been her ex-fiancé's biting comment. "I plan to keep it that way. How do you—" Now it was her turn to look him over, from broad chest to white Reeboks, and she gulped again. "—um, stay in such good shape?"

"Hey, I don't eat this way all the time—it's a treat. If you don't treat yourself, how do you know what you're missing?"

"A look at the nutrition label tells me what I'm missing." Desperate to get away—she was much too attracted to this man, no doubt a rebound effect—she grabbed a bag of chocolate covered peanuts from the rack and slapped it down next to the water. "There. Four hundred calories."

"I'm humbled," Logan told her. "You might try sprinkling them on the popcorn."

"Thank you." She shoved a fifty into Tupper's hands and told him to keep the change, which made his eyes pop. "I'll remember you on my next trip to the scales."

"Wait—" Logan held his hand out, but became distracted when Tupper called his name.

"Say, that's a great idea. Chocolate covered popcorn, M&M popcorn, popcorn with nougats—it could be the next taste sensation."

Logan held out his empty popcorn tub. "Remember that one time when I told you to use your imagination? I take it back."

Maddie took the opportunity to sneak out the door, and hurried into the blackness before Logan could catch her. If he said anything remotely connected to getting to know her better, she would melt like the hot butter he kept talking about, and the whole nightmare of dating someone connected to her work would start all over again.

Shivering, she dropped the water and candy into her purse. Balancing the popcorn in one hand, she pulled open the van's door. What a relief to be away from that man—she'd never been so instantly affected by the opposite sex before, not even her ex-fiancé. With considerable relief, she sank into the driver's seat.

Or, more accurately, she sank onto the small body that occupied the driver's seat.

Two high voices shrieked. Maddie also gave a yell and leaped out, ready to run as her imagination conjured Munchkin muggers. But her purse caught on the empty speaker post, and she managed only to spin around.

In the hazy darkness, broken by the flickering reflection from the big screen, Maddie made out two small, round sets of eyes peering at her from inside the van. In the instant that followed, she realized this was not her van and that somehow, miraculously, she still held the popcorn without a single kernel spilled.

Then a much larger body plowed into her. She slammed down onto the hard turf, while someone else fell heavily on top of her.

# CHAPTER TWO

Despite the pain of her shoulder and hip being shoved into the ground, Maddie had one clear thought—how ironic to have never been mugged in Boston, only to face an attack in rural Indiana.

No other rational thought came after she grabbed her purse for her can of pepper spray, and realized she'd reached into an empty, crumpled popcorn tub. She was vaguely aware of shouts nearby, but couldn't tell if it was friend or foe. She screamed, kicked out, clawed, and craned her neck in an attempt to bite something. There must be at least three attackers—although two of them seemed unusually small—so she knew she needed to use every trick to hold out until help arrived.

A large, heavy body kept her pinned down despite her best efforts, and after a moment she heard a low, familiar voice grunt, "Someone tried to get in the van with my kids!"

Kids?

In the low light, through a haze of dust, she could make out feet all around, with more running her way. Her attacker still grappled with her, then reached an arm around her torso to control her until it grasped a handful of breast—and froze.

At that moment Tupper's voice cried out: "Dude, that's Maddie!"

"Maddie?" Yes, that voice was very familiar. He and Maddie stilled at the same time, although she could feel his chest heave and his breath tickle her neck. "Maddie with the van just like mine?"

*Oh, no.* Maddie let go of the finger she had been about to bend backward. "Would you mind, terribly, releasing my breast?"

The weight of his body eased. "Sorry. You were—I was—uh—"

Okay—with survival no longer a concern, what was the damage? Maddie found herself sprawled on her left side, her purse crushed beneath her, and coughed from the fine dust their duel had raised. She tugged her skirt down, checked to make sure she was still buttoned up, then rolled over to push herself onto hands and knees. She felt her pantyhose rip away from one knee.

"Here, let me help you." Taking her by the waist, Logan helped Maddie to her feet. "I'm sorry—I saw somebody climb into the van with my kids, and I thought—"

"It's my fault, I thought it was my van—" She stopped as his words registered, and the red of embarrassment in her cheeks became a flush of anger. She turned back toward his van and saw a boy and girl, their tousled hair the same dark blond as Logan's, their faces glued to the window. "Are you telling me you left those children alone?"

Logan paused in the act of brushing dust from his pants. "They were supposed to lock the door behind me. They spilled the popcorn, and—"

"You left those two children out here alone in the dark, while you went away to get snacks? Are you insane? Suppose I'd been some mad psychopath, a serial killer looking for someone to victimize?" She tried to stamp her feet, but almost lost her balance because a heel had broken off.

"I'd have to wonder why you were prowling a drive-in," Logan told her in an infuriatingly mild tone.

A chuckle rose around them, and Maddie realized what must be every customer in the place surrounded them. A few began to drift away, but most seemed more interested in what developed here than the talking animals on the screen.

Logan gestured at the others. "That's the great thing about this place: These people wouldn't let something bad happen—we look out for each other."

"But to go to the theater and let perfect strangers—"

"Strangers? I've known most of those people for years. A lot of us come here every week." He turned to Tupper and added, "Anyway, this was all a misunderstanding, so we should get back to the show, right?" Taking the hint, everyone drifted away, until Maddie and Logan stood alone by his van.

When Logan reached out to touch her shoulder, Maddie stiffened from the same effect he'd had on her in the snack area, before the flying tackle. "I'm sorry about your dress."

She felt his fingers on bare skin—the sleeve of her three hundred dollar dress had separated at the seam. "You're a one man football team, aren't you?"

He shrugged. "Backup quarterback. And I'll bet you were a cheerleader."

"My school had no cheerleaders."

"Then what's the point of going?" He held up a hand against her protest. "Just kidding. Look, I really am sorry about the dress, and I'll buy you a new one."

The cost didn't bother her a bit, because her mind faded into an image of him showing up at her hotel room with a new dress, and sliding the old one off ... and not putting the new one on. Any man so passionate about protecting his children must be passionate in other areas ...

"Maddie?" Her eyes focused, and she saw his concern. "Are you all right? Did you hit your head?"

"No—no. I'm just a bit shaken up, and—and thirsty." Her mouth was dry, and not just from the dust. Remembering the water bottle, she lifted her purse.

The strap parted, and the black leather purse turned over. Water poured out, punctuated by the occasional lump of chocolate covered peanut.

Maddie glanced at Logan, who looked mortified. "You're a one man wrecking crew, that's what you are. I'll wager that's what the cheerleaders called you."

A pair of high pitched giggles punctuated the silence that followed, and they turned to see an audience of two. The oldest, a girl, called, "Now you have to get her more treats—while you refill our popcorn again!" The two collapsed onto the driver's seat, in a fit of giggles.

"They're right," Logan said. "You can send me a bill for the purse and dress, but I'll get you more popcorn and water now—it's the least I can do."

In truth, Maddie was beginning to find the whole thing amusing herself, now that she knew she wasn't about to be robbed, or worse. But she wasn't about to let him off the hook while he held that cute, embarrassed expression. "You will not leave those children alone again. That's what caused this whole incident to begin with."

"This time, *I'll* lock the door—"

"Then I'll be standing right here by the door, until you return."

"Well, they're already in their pajamas," Logan told her, as if such a comment related to the conversation. "How about this: I'll get the treats, while you sit with the kids."

He might as well ask her to sit in a pool of snakes, except she wouldn't worry about hurting the snakes. "Oh no, I couldn't possibly—"

"Oh, I'm sorry—someone must be waiting for you."

"No, I came alone, but—" Why in the world did she tell him that?

"You came alone?"

Not *that* conversation again. "Look, you don't even know me."

"I'm a good judge of character. Besides, they don't let lowlifes in here: No crooks, no lawyers, no politicians—but I repeat myself." He paused. "Get it? No? I've been practicing my jokes on kids for too long, haven't I?"

"Possibly."

"You should hear me do Dr. Seuss. Look, considering your reaction so far, you're probably the best possible person for the job." He turned to the van. "What do you think, kids? Would you like Maddie to watch the movie with us?"

What?

"Yup!" the girl yelled. The boy, who Maddie judged to be no older than five, vigorously nodded.

Maddie opened her mouth to say no. She couldn't get involved with a man here, especially a father fighting against what she was fighting for. She should, in fact, find her own van and drive away as fast as it would go.

"All right," she said.

"Great. Kids, help her get comfortable and introduce yourselves, I'll be right back." Logan trotted off toward the concession stand.

So, her impulses had betrayed her brain again. Well, she still deserved a rest. She turned to open the front door of the van, only to see the girl's round eyes seem to glow at her like an owl's.

"You have to sit in back with my dad."

Being tackled hadn't made Maddie's heart thump half this much. "Why?"

"So Conner and I can watch the movie." The girl made it sound like the most obvious thing in the world. "We can't see over your heads."

"Oh. Of course." Maddie slid open the side door and saw a small cooler dividing the bench seat. All things considered, another type of wrestling match seemed unlikely, which left her both relieved and disappointed as she sank down beside it.

She hitched her torn sleeve up, then ran a hand over the runs in her hose and wondered which muscles would be sore tomorrow, and how wise it might be to ask Logan Chandler to massage them for her, and—and why those two kids continued to stare at her.

On the driver's side, the girl had turned around to kneel on the seat, her chin on the backrest. Her brother had moved to the passenger seat and assumed the same position.

Maddie had forgotten how direct children could be. "Hello," she offered, unsure where else to start. "In all the excitement we haven't been properly introduced. I'm Maddie McKinley."

"I'm Faith Josephine McLibben Chandler, but you may call me Faith. My great-grandparents came from the Old Country. Did yours? Your name sounds like Grandma McLibben's name."

Wow. Maddie wasn't sure whether to be amused or terrified. "My great-great-great-grandparents came from the Old Country."

Faith's eyes grew even wider, if that was possible. "They must have been old."

Beside her, the boy held up one hand, fingers outstretched. "I'm five."

"He's five years old," Faith clarified, rolling her eyes. "He's very proud of that. His name is Sean Conner McLibben Chandler, but everyone calls him Conner. Would you like a sandwich?"

It took a moment for the change of subject to sink in, before Maddie's mouth started watering. "Oh, I wouldn't want to use up your food ..."

Faith rolled her eyes again. "Dad always packs too much." She reached between the seats to flip open the cooler, and Maddie saw half a dozen sandwiches wrapped in plastic.

"Too much food," Conner repeated.

Faith handed her guest a sandwich, then pointed back into the cooler. "We have apples, grapes, bananas, and nutty bars. Dad only lets us have one nutty bar a night. But we get all the popcorn we want, even if my dumb brother spills it."

"It was an accident," Conner insisted.

"I'm sure it was," Maddie assured him. "Besides, I spilled my popcorn, too."

Faith giggled. "It was funny when Dad tackled you. There's popcorn on top of the van!"

Her brother joined in the laughter. "It went all over!"

"Into the next car!"

"In dad's hair!"

"Down your dress!" Faith paused at that, looking thoughtful, then addressed Maddie with an inquisitive expression that put her on guard. "Why do you have black underwear?"

As she spoke, the van's other side door slid open. Maddie froze, sandwich poised an inch from her mouth. Logan also froze, one hand on the door and another clutching a fresh tub of popcorn. She stared involuntarily at a bulge in his jeans, then realized it was a bottle of water.

Logan followed her gaze, then yanked the bottle out of his hip pocket and held it toward her. "This is for you."

"Uh huh." She twisted the cap off and took a huge swallow, rinsing her parched mouth.

"We have pop and juice," Faith told them, sounding insulted that she didn't take something from their supply.

Logan glanced at his daughter, then climbed in, pulled the door shut, and held the bucket out to her. "Take the popcorn and watch your movie."

The kids obediently turned around, perched on pillows so they could see the screen. Behind them Maddie gave in to her hunger, and munched on the ham, lettuce, and tomato sandwich. The animated battle of good versus evil went on without her notice. She could feel Logan's gaze on her, but her somewhat infamous sharp tongue deserted her entirely. It was like being a teenager on a date again, although as a teenager she'd never shared the back seat of any vehicle.

After finishing the last bite, and washing it down with the last swallow of water, she turned to him. "I should go—"

"No." His fingers brushed her hand. "Don't."

From in front, Conner's voice drifted back: "Yeah, stay."

"That girl from Sesame Street who Daddy says is famous is in the next movie," Faith added. "And you'll miss the ads."

Maddie tilted her head. "Is that a bad thing?"

Logan shrugged. "The kids like the ads. Really, as long as you're here you might as well have company. Why go to the drive-in and leave early?"

Why indeed? She was supposed to be here for ... for some reason. And, judging by the credits rolling on the screen, accompanied by a Celine Dion song, she had yet to get her money's worth.

"Picnic!" Faith screamed, and with squeals of joy she and her brother dove into the back seat. "We need to get the food ready before the ads come on!"

Maddie found a little boy on her lap, as the children rummaged through the cooler and picked out sandwiches, fruit, and drinks. She squeezed herself against the door, desperately wishing to be anywhere else, to no avail. "Um, didn't your father just get you popcorn?"

Faith, from her seat on her father's knees, nodded. "No more popcorn until supper's done."

"You were supposed to eat earlier," Logan reminded her.

"Yeah, but we were running late and then Conner spilled the popcorn and then you tackled Maddie." Faith triumphantly yanked an apple juice box from the cooler, then shoved it into a plastic bag with her food. "Hurry, Conner, you'll miss the ads!" She vaulted back into the driver's seat.

"Okay!" Conner snapped. "You're not my boss."

"Conner." Logan tousled the boy's hair. "Manners."

"Sorry." Conner turned to Maddie. "You want an apple?"

"Yes, thank you." She took the fruit from him and almost fainted with relief when Conner climbed up front. She didn't consider herself afraid of new things, but she'd never held a boy—or a girl, for many years—and didn't plan to make it a habit. Too many bad things could happen. Had happened. Settling back against the seat, she frowned at the apple.

"It's a Red Delicious." Logan's sympathetic tone snapped her out of it. "You eat it."

"Thank you." She took a bite and discovered it was, indeed, delicious. Then she stopped short to watch Logan produce a thermos bottle, unscrew the cap, and take an experimental sniff. "Is that … coffee?"

He turned to her, smiling at her hopeful expression. "Ah! The water girl who avoids salt and butter shows her weakness, at last. Would you like some?"

Would she ever. The stuff that passed for coffee at the airport lounge should never have gotten past security. "Yes, please—"

Glancing up, she saw Faith peek over the back of the seat and shake her head violently. Sensing the movement, Logan looked up front, but by then Faith's head had already disappeared. He shrugged and poured some rich looking coffee into the thermos cup. "It's an experimental blend, I just invented it today."

"Uh oh!" Conner squeaked, but Faith's hand shot out to slap his shoulder, silencing the boy. Taking no notice, Logan held out the cup.

"Thank you." The aroma was incredible, and Maddie breathed it in hungrily. What was wrong with those kids? Anything that smelled this good couldn't be bad. She took a sip, and the brown liquid poured down her throat like hot nectar.

Unfortunately, it stayed hot. Spicy hot. Her throat burned so badly she could feel it up into her nostrils, and sucking in a breath of air didn't help.

Looking dismayed, Logan took the cup from her shaking hand. "Too much Tabasco?"

Choking, Maddie reached for her water bottle, but found it empty. In desperation she took a huge bite out of the apple, thinking as she did that it must be the first time food was ever used to wash down a drink. It didn't help, and she was reduced to waving a hand over her face to produce a breeze.

"I'm sorry—" Reaching into the cooler, Logan opened a juice box and shoved it into her hand. "It's just that so many people like hot sauce these days, I thought it was worth a try."

Busy gulping, Maddie said nothing.

"You're supposed to try the new blends yourself first, Dad," Faith scolded. "Grandma *told* you."

"You're right, she did. And scratch the Tabasco." Logan looked mortified, although Maddie had to blink tears from her eyes to see it.

"Scratch the 'basco," Conner repeated.

When Maddie could talk again, she gasped, "This is your hobby? Torturing unsuspecting people by poisoning coffee with things no sane person would add?"

"Well ... I also play softball."

"Everybody says his lemon coffee was really good," Faith put in.

"Eat your supper, the ads are about to start." Seeing she'd emptied the first one, Logan handed Maddie another juice box. "I really am sorry. I'm told I go overboard with these experiments, but I just can't stop myself."

"Well ..." Maddie held up the apple. "You did give me a last meal."

He smiled. "I'm forgiven, then?"

"As long as your next mix doesn't include pepper." Her voice seemed normal again, and the burning slowly faded. Despite herself, Maddie couldn't be upset when she saw his expression, so she added, "Now quiet down, the ads are about to start." They smiled at each other until the silver screen ahead of them lit up again, and she watched to see what could be so great about the infamous ads.

A badly animated, black and white candy bar appeared on screen, dancing through little scratches on the film. The pitchman, sounding ravenous, spoke over the old style, upbeat music: "Yum! Yum!"

Maddie swallowed and lowered her hand, apple forgotten. "That must to be forty years old."

"Fifty, I'd guess."

"But—why—"

Logan held a finger to his lips, and Maddie heard the kids follow along with the commercial, speaking the lines word for word. Lowering his voice, he turned to her. "These are the same commercials my parents watched at their age—between 'Godzilla' and 'The Love Bug'."

Maddie couldn't begin to imagine Logan as a child. "But why are they so fascinated? I mean, modern commercials, with their digital animation and flashy effects—"

Logan shook his head. "There's no heart to them. Besides, I don't let the kids watch much TV, but we come here once a week—sometimes twice. When you're young and spending time with your family, a cardboard box can be more fun than the toy that came in it."

When Maddie's job was through, there would be no more drive-in to come to. She savagely tore another chunk from the apple, and told herself they could always get a wide screen TV and some DVD's.

The next commercial featured a bunch of teenagers munching on pizza, and although it was in color, she imagined the actors now spooned applesauce in a retirement home. Then came another black and white commercial, in which mosquitoes committed suicide by picking up and lighting insect repellent. The entire Chandler family joined in, complete with sound effects as the insects dove toward their doom, and despite herself Maddie smiled.

Then came the ads for upcoming features, most of them family films. It seemed sequels or superhero teenagers were the coming thing this summer, but Maddie never wasted much time with movies. She watched the others, instead. The kids studied each ad, commented on its stars, plot or special effects, and usually begged their father to see it. In turn Logan usually agreed, but sometimes responded with a noncommittal, "We'll see".

Amazing—while everyone else in the drive-in ran back and forth to the concession stand and restrooms, Logan turned intermission into a family affair.

Then the lights dimmed, and the next movie started. Maddie felt, rather than saw, Logan shift in his seat and lean toward her, and she felt her muscles tense when he whispered in her ear.

"She's a mysterious woman who's not quite what she seems. He's a plain spoken small town boy who loves her for what's inside, instead of the appearance she projects."

Maddie turned to stare at him, and saw his eyes gleam in the flickering screen light. Was he reading her mind, or predicting the future? "How ... how do you know?"

"I looked it up on the internet. It's always a good idea to check out a movie before the kids see it."

"Oh." She allowed herself to breathe again and looked at the screen, where the stars fought over the same taxi. She had to get herself back under control. This was nothing like her—nothing like the appearance she cultivated, anyway. "It's the age old story, then. Boy meets girl."

He nodded, turning back to the screen. "I like happy endings."

"Too bad they don't exist in real life." She could feel him turn again, but left her gaze on the screen as the man and woman argued over some minor misunderstanding, then stormed off. "That's how it really goes."

"So you're the victim of a recent breakup?"

She heard the sympathy in his voice, but wasn't convinced she deserved it. She should know better than to get into the position she did, after all. "How about you?" she ventured, to avoid his question. "Aren't you separated?"

"My wife did not leave voluntarily." His voice turned frosty, so she didn't respond, knowing they'd both hit a nerve.

After a while they relaxed again, and to her surprise Maddie found herself enjoying the picture. It was no Shakespeare, but when it came to movies these days, what was? She even laughed out loud a few times, and by the time the credits rolled she wondered why she didn't take more time out to watch a movie, or just walk in the park every now and then.

Car lights switched on, and vehicles lined up to head out. Leaning forward, Logan nudged the children and got no response. "I see another video rental in our future—this is why I shouldn't worry so much about previewing the second feature. Well, since Faith's too tired to drive home, I'd better get her back where she belongs."

They both exited the side doors at the same time and Maddie, wanting to get this over with, met him at the front of the van. "I truly appreciate your hospitality—"

"I'd like to see you again."

That was straightforward enough, and deserved a straightforward answer. "No." She saw the disappointment in his eyes, and steeled herself against it.

"Why?"

There was nothing like the truth. "Because I just got out of a hurtful relationship, and I can't afford to expose those wounds again."

"I wouldn't hurt you."

"I might make you."

Logan cocked his head. "You have your own mystery, don't you? You could give our movie heroine a run for her money."

"And you could be as dangerous as—whoever that guy was. But we're not actors, and we could really be hurt, and I'd rather leave this with a few pleasant memories—and bruises."

He smiled, a sad smile. "I won't see you again."

"Maybe we'll run into each other at the movies." She started to reach out, then turned and walked away. Maybe it wasn't the hardest thing she'd ever done, but it came close, and all the way to her own van she lectured herself on the difference between possibilities and realities.

At some point in the future, like it or not, she would be this man's enemy, and any further involvement would make the future that much more painful. Besides, she'd sworn to never involve herself with kids again, and how could she fall for him without falling for his two darling children, too? No, it was better this way.

She climbed into the van, and found it so jarringly like his that she determined to get rid of it as soon as possible. She'd come here to prove herself, which meant not needing another man—not needing anyone. Banging her fists against the wheel didn't help, so she took a deep breath, then reached for the key.

A key that was already on.

For four hours the van had sat unlocked, with the key in the ignition—it was a miracle it was still there. Maddie stared at the dark dashboard. She'd left the radio on; why wasn't it still? Impending doom enveloped her as she reached forward and turned the key.

Nothing happened.

"Well, of course." She turned to see another van disappear around the wooden fence that surrounded the property. His started just fine, thank you. Seeing the rest of the lot empty and silent, she reached into her purse for her cell phone.

Her hand contacted something wet and squishy. She pulled out a dripping candy box, then reached back in and found a cell phone which, no surprise, wouldn't work.

So much for needing no one.

Then she heard the deep rumble of an engine start, and two headlights shone out from behind the concession stand. Her grip on the steering wheel tightened—she was alone out here.

An ancient tow truck emerged and rattled forward, threatening to shake apart every time it crested the little hills that lined the lot. It rumbled to a stop in front of her, and on the side of the white truck she saw tattered red lettering: "Mallie's All Night Towing".

To Maddie's surprise, a woman cranked open the driver's side window, a familiar looking young woman with bright green, spiked hair. "Uncle Mallie said I'd find work here—some batteries don't make it all the way through two features."

Then someone sitting beside the green haired girl leaned forward, to give Maddie a thumb's up. "Mallie—Maddie. It's like karma, huh?"

Maddie sighed, then reached down to pull the hood latch. "You're a bad penny, Tupper."

"Huh?"

"That means, thank you." But while Tupper and his girlfriend prepared to jump start the van's battery, it occurred to Maddie that here were more people she was destined to disappoint.

# CHAPTER THREE

"What happened to me?"

Maddie rolled over and jammed a pillow over her ears, but the unsympathetic alarm clock kept on beeping.

"How could I lose all my dignity so quickly?" She sat up and slapped the clock, then gazed around the dark hotel room.

Well, wasting time on despair was pointless. Throwing the covers aside, Maddie stood and, happily, discovered only a few sore muscles. She'd seek out a local fitness center, and be ready the next time a strong, sexy, rock hard man who wore a hint of Old Spice decided to tackle her.

She needed a shower. A cold one.

Maddie marched across the room and turned on the overhead light. It chased the darkness away, but revealed her dress in an unstylish pile where she'd thrown it against the bathroom door the previous night. One leg of her shredded pantyhose lay draped over the side of a trash can, and next to it were her ruined shoes.

At least the dress appeared to be salvageable. She'd only brought five pair of the expensive, designer brand pantyhose, and there'd be no saving this pair.

When she picked up the dress, one sleeve fell off. Any further question about whether the outfit could be saved was answered when she noticed the grass stains on the back and side, glaring through a layer of dust. So, she'd lost every article of clothing she'd worn that night, except for the black underwear Logan's kids were probably still talking about.

"John Adams never got tackled at the drive-in." She scooped the sleeve up, shoved the whole mess into the trash can, then changed her mind when she thought about the maid service and instead dumped the ensemble on the bed, so she could hide it in her luggage later.

Her first souvenir of the trip. And, maybe, her happiest memory—despite the fact that her entire image, the image she'd built up in everyone's minds all her adult life, had been shredded as badly as her hosiery.

"I'm chic. I am." She opened the closet door to get a look at herself in the full length mirror. In her exhaustion, she'd forgotten to change into her nightgown—or even open her suitcases to retrieve one. Hardnosed lawyers did not go to bed clad only in black lace.

"But I *am* chic," she reminded her reflection, which looked completely unconvinced. "I'm buff. I wear Victoria's Secret, but only I know it, so I feel womanly yet businesslike in—I'm talking to myself."

Who was she trying to convince? Maybe that woman in the mirror, who looked not sexy but vulnerable standing there in her underwear, whose hair was mussed and tangled, whose shoulder and hip sported fresh bruises from contact with the hard earth. Who looked, in other words, like the scared child from so long ago, who couldn't handle responsibility.

Maddie closed the door, shut out the frightened youth, and started her transformation.

In the shower she refused to think of Logan Chandler, or anything except clearing her mind for the day ahead. She left the bathroom long enough to haul in a case of what would look to a man like torture devices, with which she turned her blonde mane from a tangled mess into waves that lay just so, to frame her face and fall across her shoulders. Makeup—but not too much—designed to make her look as if she could be perfect without wearing any. And a little bit extra over the shoulder bruise. Then a dash of Coco Chanel.

She moved back into the spacious bedroom and opened her suitcases. Without knowing how anyone she met today could affect her job, she was determined to look professional, yet feminine enough to give whoever she opposed a false sense of her ability. Last night notwithstanding, she was here to do a job, and all's fair in corporate warfare.

With a wince at the memory of a little girl's innocent question, Maddie chose white underwear, the plain Jane kind. She opened her second pair of Sheer Invites hosiery, and wondered how hard it would be to find a local shop that carried them. Well, there was always online shopping. After an impatient wait for the Weather Channel's forecast, she zipped on a pastel yellow sleeveless dress, also silk. Only when finished did Maddie check herself again in the mirror.

There. Completely professional, completely in control. Having once again shoved the scared little girl into a dark part of her subconscious, she donned matching pumps, walked into the suite's outer room, and pushed open the curtain.

Two floors below she saw the same parking lot, then the same highway, that she'd see from any hotel room in the country. Past that—the same fast food establishments and convenience stores. There was no way to judge the town of Hopewell, Indiana, or its people, from this relatively new development on the northern outskirts. By all accounts, it was Hopewell where most of the resistance to the new airport originated.

She double checked her maps and the fact sheet her assistant had prepared for her. The town of less than nine thousand rested in a valley, only a few miles north of the drive-in. In fact, the whole area around the drive-in was prime real estate, situated between Hopewell and the fast growing north side of Fort Wayne. What backward fringe group wouldn't want the benefits a major development would bring to their community? First task: Check out the downtown and identify her enemies.

At least she had a spacious suite with enough room to set up a temporary office. She hoped it wouldn't come to that, but her visit to the drive-in had convinced her a little crafty arm twisting wouldn't be enough to solve the problem, this time.

As she reached the door her dried-out cell phone rang, a miraculous noise—considering its misadventure the night before—that annoyed her all the same. "Hello?"

"Hey, sweetie!"

"Dena, you are my personal assistant, and thus an employee. Please don't refer to me as 'sweetie'. Besides, it's undignified." Despite her words, Maddie couldn't stop smiling as she punched the elevator button. Dena had that effect on people.

"Sorry—grandma. You're such an old fussbudget." Dena's high, musical voice held a hint of laughter, as usual. She was just a few years younger than Maddie, but Maddie thought of her as a kind of female Peter Pan, someone who refused to get serious no matter what the world threw at her. "I expected to hear from you last night."

Maddie held the door open for an elderly couple who apparently traveled with all their worldly possessions, then punched the lobby button. "I assumed you'd be at your dance class."

"Tonight's the dance class—last night, karate. So, how was the trip?"

"Bumpy, and getting bumpier. Do you know about this kid who was supposed to be doing the prep work here?"

"Just that he's related to Big Boss, and also to the guy who owns the development company—which means those two are related to each other. Go figure, huh?"

"Yes, indeed." That explained a lot about how the firm got involved with a development plan in Indiana to begin with. "He doesn't know why I'm here, and his only prep work was the hotel room, a rental van, and a list of every tourist attraction in the tristate area."

"A van?"

"I miss my Porsche. I want my Porsche."

The elderly couple beside her grinned, and the woman laid a hand on Maddie's arm. "There's nothing like a fast car, dear. Herbert won me over with a 1949 MG."

Herbert nodded vigorously. "It's such a part of our history that when it couldn't be fixed we rustproofed it, parked it in the back yard, filled the seat with earth, and planted lilies."

"That's original." The image struck Maddie so vividly that when the couple got off she almost forgot to follow. She heard Dena giggle.

"They're both wearing Hawaiian shirts, tan shorts and white socks, aren't they?"

It was always hard to tell whether Dena's insights were a psychic vision or a good guess. "Right as usual," Maddie told her, as she stopped by a coffee pot in the lobby. "I need coffee. Real coffee. Do they have Starbucks in Indiana?"

"You're still in the States, you know."

"I take your point." Trying to be discreet, Maddie stepped closer to the pot and sniffed, then turned a determined stride toward the front door. "That is *so* not real coffee."

Clouds obscured the rising sun, and Maddie thought she would be safe from wilting for another few hours. But all thoughts of weather or caffeine fled when she glanced at a paper box and saw the headline:

AIRPORT OPPONENTS ORGANIZE

"Oh, my."

"What? Don't tell me you're having problems already. You didn't fall for some corn fed Hoosier boy, did you?"

Maddie almost dropped the phone. "In one night?"

"I forgot, you don't believe in anything you can't see or touch." *Definite scoffing in Dena's tone.* "The rumor mill is working overtime about you being exiled to Indiana, so if you plan to make partner you'd better—"

"And why does the rumor mill say I'm exiled?" Maddie dug into her purse—what man would think to bring a backup purse?—for change, and tried to ignore the heat rising in her face.

"Maddie, you were engaged to a partner and now you're not. Need I say more?"

"What? No 'I told you so'?" With some difficulty, Maddie managed to hold onto the phone and pull out a newspaper at the same time. She unfolded it on top of the paper box, and almost didn't hear Dena's next words.

"And hit you when you're down? Why don't you quit here and go someplace where they appreciate your ability as a lawyer, instead of your skill at throwing drinks in a man's face?"

"I don't quit." Maddie scanned the article, her part of the

40

conversation on automatic, as if they'd had it before—which they had. "My personal life shouldn't impact my professional life."

"And yet it did, so spectacularly. Throwing a drink in a man's face is a time honored tactic, but you should maybe throw just the martini, not the martini and the glass, and the olive. Which got stuck in his nose. In front of all the other partners. Are you still there?"

"We've got problems." She folded the paper back up and hurried toward the van.

"At least they were able to get the olive out. Are we talking about the same problems?"

"There's more opposition to this airport than we were led to believe. It's not just the owner, it's the whole community, and the development company tried to steamroll it through without public support." She unlocked the van and climbed in, her mind racing. "Business law isn't my area of expertise, as I repeatedly tried to tell Quincy when he sent me here, and this won't be the cakewalk he insinuated. I need you to meet with him and tell him I need support."

Dena apparently recognized Maddie's all business voice, a voice Maddie had practiced since law school. "I'll never get past his outer office, but I'll try. They won't send another attorney, though."

"Surely they wouldn't sabotage this whole deal just to make me look foolish?"

"Not on purpose, maybe. But they know your ability—it's your loyalty they're testing. If you can't do this, your career is in big trouble."

"Thank you, Miss Obvious." Unbelievable, that her ex-fiancé would convince the company to endanger a multimillion dollar deal out of spite. But logic often fled in the face of emotions. "I've got to go check out the town, and find a good coffee house. Please do what you can—Tupper's loyal, but so is a Labrador Retriever, and that won't help

41

me now."

"Tupper—? Never mind. I'll blow a bugle and find the cavalry."

Maddie disconnected and pulled out into traffic, headed for the downtown area she'd bypassed the night before. It didn't take long to reach. She drove up and down the main drag twice, searching for a familiar coffee chain, before she thought to check her phone. It turned out Hopewell had no familiar coffee chain.

Hopewell was split by a four lane Main Street, lined with two and three story brick buildings for several blocks. She made note of City Hall, the library, a chamber of commerce office, and a two screen theater, all near the middle of town. The rest of the businesses were small shops: the expected mix of drug, clothing, hardware, and specialty stores.

She doubled back through side streets, but only on her third, and increasingly desperate, trip up Main did she spot a sign with the magic word: "Coffee". The bright blue and white shop held a good corner location, with a fire escape snaking up the side to an upstairs office area. Although Maddie wasn't familiar with the name, she got an immediate good feeling about it. Maybe she could grab breakfast there, but first things first.

She had trouble finding a parking space, but took that as a good sign. A vital, bustling downtown encouraged growth, which in turn would encourage services like a local airport, which made the development that much more logical. She hurried into the shop with visions of heavily caffeinated ecstasy dancing in her head.

It was like stepping back half a century. A bell rang on the door, and people who occupied half the tables paused in their conversation to look up with curious, but friendly, smiles. To Maddie's left, a counter stretched along the wall. The tables, which looked out over downtown through plate glass, took up the rest of the room.

"Are you all right, little lady?" a man wearing overalls asked, half rising. Maddie turned to him, wondering just how out of place she appeared, but then he gestured at her arm. "You're pretty bruised up."

So she hadn't used enough makeup, making the whole sleeveless dress concept a poor idea. "Thank you, I'm fine—I had a mishap yesterday."

A woman at the next table cooed sympathetically. "Accidents will happen."

Next to the first speaker, another man, who wore a dark suit and tie, nodded. "At least you didn't get tackled at the drive-in." The entire room erupted into laughter.

Oh, Lord. The story had traveled the state already. Maddie abandoned her plan to sit down and instead moved to the counter, determined to get a cup of java to go. At first she saw no one, but as she tried to peek through the swinging doors behind the counter they burst open, and a short, thin waitress hurried through.

At least, Maddie assumed it was the waitress until she took a closer look. They both froze, staring at each other.

"Maddie!" Faith Chandler slammed against the counter, grinning with the kind of genuine pleasure only a ten-year-old could exhibit without embarrassment. "It *is* you!"

"Faith? But—" Maddie sank onto a stool, her head spinning. What was the employment age here? Where was the adult supervision? Never mind that—what kind of karmic jokester pulled this trick off? "It's good to see you again." But she glanced around for somebody else.

Behind her, the room fell silent. Just as that fact penetrated, a force hit her from the side, and two small arms encircled her waist. "Maddie! You came back!"

"Yes, I did." She reached down to tousle Conner's hair, not that it needed help being unruly. "But I didn't know you two were here. Has your father put you to work to pay for that popcorn?"

"Conner's supposed to be wiping tables." Faith's smile turned into a frown.

"I had to go," Conner protested.

"Faith Chandler, you're being too hard on him!" a man called from one of the tables.

Beside him, a young pastor in a wheelchair added, "The tables are all wiped, Faith."

Maddie looked behind her, and knew by the sly smiles and low chuckles that people were putting two and two together. "It looks like he did a very nice job cleaning up, Faith."

Conner beamed at her, but Maddie was still looking around for an adult employee. "Um ... do you two work here?"

"Kind of." The little girl took a cup from under the counter. "Would you like some coffee?"

"Regular black, please." As soon as the words spilled automatically from her mouth, Maddie wanted to yank them back. She'd be responsible if the little girl was burned—but Faith poured the coffee like an experienced professional. What was going on here? Logan seemed like such a caring father, but left his kids alone in the van, and now they ran a shop by themselves. She looked around again, and noticed hand drawn pictures secured by magnets to the side of a refrigerator, then a portrait of the children on a wall. What in the world?

Faith carefully placed the cup before Maddie. "We have a special on the cinnamon rolls; my grandma makes them herself."

"That would be very nice. Is your grandma here?"

"She's in the back with Aunt Lydia, making more rolls."

Aha. A copy of the shop's outside sign hung from a wall, and this time Maddie took in all the words: "Chandler's House of Coffee". Not original, but descriptive. How would she have reacted if she'd put it all together before walking in?

Conner released Maddie and ran around to the back of the counter, where he dished out a roll while Maddie lifted the coffee cup, then hesitated. "Um ... this isn't a special blend, is it?"

Faith shook her head. "Just regular beans. Grandma won't let any of the specials be served here until Dad tastes them himself."

Fresh ... strong ... Maddie took a sip, and almost fainted with pleasure—the real deal. "Faith, this is delicious."

"Thank you." Faith leaned forward, with the expression of someone imparting national secrets. "I don't really drink coffee. But Grandma says this is so good because Daddy blends it himself."

"Maybe he should have stopped with this, before someone got hurt." Faith giggled.

The doorbell jangled, and what little whispered conversation still went on ceased so abruptly that Maddie turned to look. A sandy haired man stood in the doorway, wearing slacks, a light blue dress shirt with matching tie, and an expression of disbelief. While he stared at Maddie, the door swung closed behind him and almost knocked the briefcase he carried out of his hand.

After a moment of silence a uniformed police officer in the back of the room stood up, deposited his cup on the counter, sauntered to the door, then stabbed a finger at Logan's chest. "Ma'am—is this the man who assaulted you?"

The room erupted in laughter.

45

Maddie sipped her coffee, pretending to consider the matter. "Well, it was dark ... but if he's been telling the story then yes, he must be the one."

The officer nodded and turned to Logan. "I think you owe this lady breakfast, or I'll have to run you in." With a parting salute, he strode out the door.

Logan walked toward Maddie, but got ambushed by customers calling questions and comments. She continued to stare at him, wondering how any man could be so attractive this early in the morning, especially with off the shelf clothes. His nimble fingers loosened the tie, making him look somehow even sexier.

A small hand tapped on her shoulder, and she turned to see Conner on the stool beside her. He pointed to a steaming cinnamon roll, covered with icing, on a plate before her. "That's yours."

Faith held out a fork. Maddie took it, then turned to her left to see Logan, elbow propped on the counter, regarding her with that perfect smile. She was surrounded.

"How did you find us?" Logan asked.

"I was looking for coffee." Maddie brandished her cup.

"Fate, then." He looked pleased at the possibility.

"I don't believe in fate. Or karma, or serendipity, or anything else I can't reach out and touch." She'd made that comment many times before, but it was hard to chalk this one up to coincidence.

"But you came looking for coffee, and I make the best coffee in the Midwest." She felt the warmth of his fingers when Logan reached out to touch her hand. "You can touch that, can't you?"

"Murphy works in mysterious ways."

Frowning, Faith looked from one adult to the other. "Who's Murphy?"

"Murphy is a guy who makes up all sorts of strange laws," her father explained. "The most famous one is, 'Whatever can possibly go wrong, will'."

Maddie nodded. "Murphy's law of coincidence is, 'when two people are least likely to run into each other, they will'."

"Not fate?" Logan paused to wave at a departing customer, then did a double take when he saw it was the wheelchair bound pastor. "Jake, do you believe in fate?"

"Absolutely. There's a plan, and that plan does not involve throwing down on strange women at the theater. See you Sunday."

Logan frowned at him, but the pastor just winked and went on, so Logan turned his attention back to Maddie. "You think when two people, who by rights should never see each other again, suddenly meet in this big world, it's coincidence?"

"That's what coincidence is." Maddie sipped her coffee, and searched for a way to change the subject. All her life she'd worked for what she wanted, refusing to believe chance held any power over will, but since she'd come to Indiana that commitment toward rational thinking had taken quite a beating. "You know, I'm covered with bruises." There, that would change the subject.

Logan's gaze raked her body, making Maddie shiver. Okay, time for another subject change.

"It's on this side, Dad," Conner pointed out.

"Her arm is black and blue," Faith agreed.

"Well ..." Logan glanced toward the tables, now mostly empty. "The least I can do is buy you breakfast. We don't have a big selection, but you'll love that roll."

Maddie's stomach agreed with a rumble. "Fair enough."

Before she knew it, Maddie found herself sitting at a round table near the back of a coffee shop, with two children and a man who made more than her bruises ache. The cinnamon roll, she discovered, was as good as advertised, and each of them polished one off.

As they ate, other customers drifted in, and when the swinging doors to the back room opened Maddie looked up, anxious to see what this crew's matriarch was like. To her surprise, the woman who bustled through the door was black; it turned out "Aunt" Lydia was an employee, rather than a blood relative. Lydia exchanged introductions with Maddie, then shot her a curious look before disappearing again into the back room.

"You need another cup of coffee," Logan announced as he dabbed a napkin to his lips. "What do you think, Conner? The new almond mix?"

Conner looked shocked. "But Dad, that's still s'perimental."

But Faith solemnly climbed to her feet. "Dad's tried it. It's time to test it on someone else."

Maddie felt like she was the subject of a chemistry experiment, but when Faith presented her with the cup, even though she usually stuck with plain black, she didn't hesitate. A touch of almond teased her tongue, and cinnamon, and by the second swallow she knew she was experiencing something magical. "How did you manage a blend like this?"

"I kidnapped Juan Valdez." The kids, clearly familiar with the joke, giggled.

Maddie's smile froze when Logan spoke again. "So, what brings you to northeast Indiana?"

She must tell the truth. She couldn't lead this wonderful man on any longer. She couldn't let his children grow attached, only to be told later she was some kind of monster. Straight up and honest, as she'd always sworn to be, in the face of her profession's reputation.

"I'm doing research." Okay, true enough. Keep going.

Logan looked interested. "What sort of research?"

"On small town life." What? "I'm researching how rural people think and feel in ways different from big city residents, and how it affects their opinions on economic issues."

Logan nodded. "You work for a college?"

"No, I represent the industry." What industry? "My area of expertise is the family, and its relation to the community." *Family law. Say family law!*

"That's interesting," Logan said, seeming to mean it. It didn't seem so interesting to the kids, who, without being asked, started clearing tables of breakfast clutter. "As it happens, I just got back from a meeting that relates to the effect of economic growth on families."

*Oh, no.* "Oh. Yes?"

"I'm on the Chamber of Commerce, and we're fighting a proposed airport near town." Logan's eyes took on a frightening intensity. "Actually, we parked in the middle of it last night."

"The drive-in," Maddie murmured.

"Exactly."

Maddie sipped her coffee and looked outside, where steady traffic passed on the city streets, and pedestrians walked to and from local businesses. She compared that to the vast, empty fields around the drive-in, and couldn't see how a community leader could justify Logan's point of view. At the risk of upsetting him, she decided to probe further. "Wouldn't the local economy benefit more from an airport than from a drive-in?"

"On paper, yes." To her relief, Logan didn't seem angry, but he tensed and leaned forward. "I practically grew up at that drive-in: I saw my first movie there, and stole my first kiss there, and met my wife there." He faltered for a moment, then went on with renewed determination. "The same is going for my kids, but this isn't about nostalgia. That place has been in one family from the day it was built, and the owner doesn't want to sell a place his father put so much of his life and fortune into. He shouldn't be forced out because someone else covets his land."

"You know the owner?"

"He was my dad's sergeant in Vietnam." Logan sat back, but did not relax. "My father taught me big business may be the muscle of America, but small business is America's heart."

So. It was personal. Maddie wanted to bridge the gap between his views and her job, but it grew wider whenever they spoke, and she didn't know what to do about it. It didn't help that she saw his point, because she was still being paid to argue the other side—and it wouldn't be the first time a lawyer fought for something they didn't personally believe in.

A penny landed on the table between them, then spun lazily to a stop.

Maddie looked from it to him, and saw Logan smile. "Penny for your thoughts," he said. "It's impolite to leave without saying goodbye."

"I was thinking that, as a businessman, you should be more interested in your personal economy than in someone else's business."

"Possibly." He shrugged. "Certainly it's been a rough fight—we're even looking for someone to rent the office above my shop, to help pay legal fees. If you ever need to set up an office in Hopewell, look us up."

She gave him a weak smile. That would be the last place she'd want to establish a base—it would be like camping in the middle of an enemy fort.

"My father also taught me all the little guys need to stick together when it comes to battling the big guys. Besides, a community's health has to do with more than traffic flow and tax base. Sometimes it's atmosphere, and history, and spirit."

At that moment Maddie knew she could never change Logan's mind, and her best bet would be to do her job, get out, and forget this man and his city.

"My tip!" Conner yelled, grabbing up the coin before turning to Maddie. "You hafta eat with us."

"I just did eat with you."

Shaking her head, Faith joined her brother by the table. "He means, you have to eat dinner with us, at our house tonight."

The thought sent a stake through Maddie's heart, which was appropriate, since she was starting to feel like a vampire prowling around her victims. "Why?"

"Because Grandma went to work at the food bank, but she says she wants to meet you because you're all Daddy talked about today."

Conner nodded. "So you hafta eat with us."

Maddie swallowed and turned to their father, who watched her with his mouth quirked and one eyebrow raised. "You can't argue with that."

"But I—"

"If you knew my mother, you'd understand you really can't argue with that."

Maddie sighed, looking from one hopeful expression to another. She should feel flattered—apparently they saw something in her she didn't see herself—but instead fought exasperation. This would get her nowhere. This would cause nothing but trouble. This—

This would be the perfect opportunity to find out what the other side was planning.

Maddie didn't want to hurt these people, but her career was on the line. Harvard taught her the law, but the firm of Quincy, Dixon and Tremayne taught her how to win, which included using any tactic the law allowed. At any other time she wouldn't hesitate to take this opportunity, and she couldn't respect herself if she didn't take it now.

"I'd be happy to have dinner with you tonight," she said. Over the childish cheers that followed, she realized she might not be able to come out with her self-respect intact, no matter what path she followed.

# CHAPTER FOUR

Logan Chandler considered himself a calm, cool man.

Not cool in the teenage, perfect hair and stylish clothes kind of way. Even-tempered. Not prone to jump into things blindly. Or so he'd always thought, until he caught himself primping in his bedroom mirror while awaiting the arrival of a woman he barely knew.

He glanced out the window, pretending to examine the tops of Hopewell's downtown buildings from over the neighborhood maple trees three blocks away. That wasn't what he was really looking for.

Clearly he was fooling himself with that level headed self-image. It was a demeanor practiced and perfected ever since his football days, when losing his temper almost landed him in jail.

Logan paused in the middle of pulling on his favorite sweater, a dark green knit, and shuddered. How long—fifteen years ago? He closed his eyes and saw his friend on a stretcher, while he raged against the player who put him there.

For weeks he brooded about it, until a young woman dragged him out of his black mood. His injured friend became the pastor of their church, and the young woman became Logan's wife.

The photo on Logan's dresser showed a beauty with freckles and long ringlets of flame red hair, eternally twenty-seven. She'd taught him all the important lessons in his life: To love, to trust, and to keep a punching bag in the basement for those times when life got to be too much.

Good advice for a widowed father who liked to get involved in lost causes.

Logan turned to head downstairs, but stopped with his hand on the doorknob. What would Lise think of Maddie McKinley? An unfair question, but in the five years since his wife's death this was the first woman to have any impact on him. Was she that special, or was he getting past the pain, or some combination of both?

He wished he could speak with his wife. If only he'd seen the signs, made sure she got diagnosed sooner—

With a shake of his head, Logan opened the door and headed down the hallway. He'd long ago learned to stop worrying about what he couldn't change, and concentrate on what he could.

At the top of the stairs he leaned against the railing to survey the living room. The kids had pushed the coffee table against the picture window, which looked out over the front porch, and pretended to color while peeking through the half closed curtain. Like father, like kids.

Faith and Conner fell for Maddie even faster than Logan, and that worried him. He'd had no chance to find out how long Maddie planned to stay in the area, but she was obviously a professional who wasn't about to drop her job to settle down in small town Indiana. Who did she work for—what did she even do? He could survive getting involved and then losing again, but a breakup would hit his children hard.

Since the moment she entered their lives there had been little choice in the matter, or so it seemed. She looked so lost there at the drive-in, even before he gave her the flying tackle, that he couldn't leave her alone in her van. And showing up at the shop—who could imagine such a thing? Add that to his mother, who said she wanted to meet Maddie but then had to run off before she could, and it did seem fate kept pushing them together.

Conner dropped his crayon and shot to his feet, staring through the window. "Wow."

His sister looked up, then also stood and leaned so far forward she seemed ready to pitch forward. "Wow."

"Is she an angel?" Conner gasped.

"No." But Faith sounded doubtful. "Mommy's an angel. She's just ... wow." Then the two waved, and dashed to the front door.

*Interesting.* Logan forced himself to walk down the stairs, feeling his heart thump with every step, and made it halfway down before his children jerked the door open to reveal Maddie on the porch.

Wow.

She wore some kind of wispy silk outfit, which swept in layers to just below her knees. Its rainbow colors were tucked in folds over her shoulders, but left the pale, perfect skin of her neck exposed. She'd gathered her blonde hair into some impossibly complicated pattern, leaving a few strategically placed strands to fall across her ears.

Maddie knelt down to greet the shouting children, and Logan noticed the sheen of hosiery and strapless high heels. He'd invited her to a meal at his home—hadn't he? There wasn't a single place in town ritzy enough for that outfit.

After a moment Maddie stood and glanced around, then spotted Logan poised on the stairs. She regarded him with hands on hips, which accentuated gentle curves and brought a lump to his throat. "You're quite handsome tonight, Mr. Chandler."

He glanced down at his sweater and dark slacks. "I feel like I'm wearing greasy overalls, or at least jeans and a T-shirt." He had to remind his feet to continue on down the stairs.

"So I'm Sandy and you're my Danny Zukko?"

With a shout of joy, Faith jumped up and down. "I love 'Grease'!"

Maddie patted the girl on her shoulder. "I saw it on Broadway a few years ago."

Faith stilled, her eyes wide. "You saw the play? We did too, at the high school."

"That's a little off Broadway," Logan added. "But still a quality production."

"I'm sure." Maddie's eyes sparkled as she discussed the show with Faith. Logan wondered again at the way Maddie was so good with kids, but at the same time seemed afraid of them. Maybe it was just that she had none of her own—or did she? He knew so little about Maddie. His mother would change that, if she was to maintain her reputation.

He wondered if he should warn Maddie about—

Too late. The door to the kitchen burst open and his mother, wearing her signature flowered dress, burst through. Her hair, now mostly gray, was held back in a bun, and she wore a white apron with the lettering, "Pay the Cook".

"There now, you lightning bugs stand back and give our guest some room—wow." She stopped in her tracks—something Logan rarely saw—and looked Maddie up and down. "Aren't you gussied up?"

"She's like an angel," Conner explained.

"I had a limited number of outfits," Maddie said, with a gesture at the dress. "I know I'm overdressed, but—"

"Nonsense!" Hurrying forward again, Logan's mother took

56

Maddie by the arm and led her into the living room. "I'm Judy Chandler, and you're welcome in our home no matter what you're wearing. Besides, my son probably ruined all the rest of your clothes."

"Wait a minute." Logan held a finger up in protest. "Just one outfit—"

"And the only one she had for a gathering like this." Judy led Maddie to the couch and gestured for the children. "Lightning bugs, would you keep Maddie company for a moment while your dad helps me in the kitchen?"

The kids loudly agreed. Logan tried to protest, but Judy, whose head barely came to his shoulders, slapped his arm as she passed, and kept going. He followed her into the kitchen, where he found the table set and ready. "What—"

"You did tell her we would eat here?" Judy gave her son an accusing glare.

"Of course I did—"

"And that it was casual?"

"How else would you dress, eating at someone's home?"

"How would you dress for dinner at the White House?" She gave him a triumphant glare, then turned to check a pot on the stove. "And that's someone's house, isn't it?"

Logan suspected Maddie could wear cutoff blue jeans and a tank top and still look classy, not to mention sexy, but he wasn't about to tell his mother that.

"Of course," Judy added without turning around, "it makes you wonder why a researcher traveling to a small town packs formal wear."

"Well, maybe our idea of casual wear isn't the same as in the big city."

"And what city is she from?"

Good question. "Um ... the big one."

Now Judy turned around, holding a ladle out like a sword. "Shouldn't you know?"

"It never came up."

"Don't you think you should know something about a woman who'll be spending time around your home and children?"

Time? Logan rarely considered the future, beyond college funds or saving the drive-in. Then he wondered if the drive-in was more about the past. "I never said—"

"You said everything." Her eyes softening, Judy put the ladle back in a pot and gave her son a hug. "You said everything when you talked about her all morning, just the day after you met. You said everything when you asked the kids what they thought of her." Then she pulled away and added, "It's easy to tell you're attracted to this woman, which is a good thing, but make sure you know her well. After all, you married your high school sweetheart, so you don't have a lot of experience in dating."

That couldn't be denied. "So, what do you think of her?"

"Why, I came here to watch my grandchildren, not you! Besides, I just met her myself. Now get in there and entertain, while I finish up."

Logan started toward the living room, but paused in the hallway when he spotted the wedding photo on the wall. He looked at his wife, so young and joyful, and murmured, "What do *you* think of her?"

He could swear Lise winked at him, a habit whenever she was in a playful mood, but he chalked it up to the flickering candle his mother had lit in the hallway.

Maddie, it appeared, needed rescuing. She sat on the center of the couch with a child glued to either side, and examined newly colored pictures as Faith and Conner passed them back and forth. But she did appear more comfortable than their first meeting, so Logan paused in the doorway to watch them.

"I like the color in this one," Maddie said as she took another page.

"I did the green and blue," Faith told her.

"I did the red," Conner added. "I stayed in the lines."

Maddie nodded, as serious as the five year old beside her. "Yes, you did. And it's important to know how to stay between the lines, but what if you took this blank space in the corner and drew something there? You could make your own lines, then color them in."

Conner stared down at the paper, his mouth forming a silent O. Then he took the page back and reached for a pencil.

Instead of leaving Maddie's lap bare, Faith dropped another page onto it. "I don't color much, but this one reminded me of you."

Now Maddie's mouth dropped. Intrigued by her reaction, Logan stepped forward so he could see the page.

It showed a princess, standing in front of a castle. The dress was longer than the one Maddie wore, but otherwise it, and the princess' hairstyle, looked remarkably similar to hers. Faith had covered it with bright flowers, and colored the hair yellow, then used a blue crayon to write "Maddie" on the top of the page.

Logan had trouble catching his breath. True, Faith rarely colored now, considering it beneath her age level. And since her mother's death, she'd never colored a woman's hair anything but red.

As if sensing his presence, Maddie looked up. "Look. Isn't it lovely?"

Unable to trust his voice, Logan nodded. Twenty-four hours after meeting Maddie McKinley, his kids were falling for her—and so was he.

His mother was right. He had to know more about Maddie, before something turned up to break their hearts.

Maddie stared in dismay at the plate in front of her.

Pork chops, mashed potatoes heaped with gravy, green beans, a huge dinner roll. In the center of the table stood the most luscious looking apple pie she could ever imagine.

There were more calories on this one plate than she consumed in a week.

Judy, to her credit, seemed understanding. From her seat at an oak table so big a Lazy Susan in its center passed the food around, she waved at their guest. "It's all right, dear. I know it's not tofu and sprouts, but trust me when I say you're a little underweight—at least, by Indiana standards."

Maddie glanced at Logan, who dished up a plate for Conner and, she assumed, pretended he hadn't heard the comment. True, more than one person tried to be "helpful" by informing Maddie she was skinny. Certainly she could use more weight on her chest, which, as Logan discovered, was barely a handful. Besides, Judy presumably ate this way all the time, and seemed healthier than any other elderly person Maddie had ever seen.

"All right—I'll have the sprouts tomorrow." She took a bite of mashed potatoes, a dish she'd avoided for ten years, and almost melted into the chair. "This is—this is—"

"Homemade," Logan supplied.

When did Maddie last eat anything homemade? At what point in her life did she conclude eating at a five star restaurant every night could somehow be better than this? "Yes, homemade, but definitely better than my home."

"That reminds me, dear," Judy said as she cut her pork chop, "I never caught where your home is."

Maddie fleetingly wondered if the truth would connect her with the developer. But she couldn't imagine how, and thankfully didn't have to be misleading. "Boston."

Judy froze, a fork halfway to her mouth. Across the table, Logan choked on his food and had to grab for his glass of iced tea. It didn't take a Harvard degree to tell Maddie had said something wrong. Had the development opponents discovered a Boston law firm was involved?

"Boston, dear?" Judy shot her son a pointed look. "Do you live near the Big Dig, by any chance?"

"No." It surprised Maddie to find Hoosiers knew of the massive underground roadway project. Then again, the job got a lot of press. "I have a place a mile or so away."

Logan carefully set his glass down. "So, you don't live near the downtown throughway?" His voice sounded tightly controlled.

"No, I like to stay away from the traffic." Why did her home's location seem so important to them?

Both Logan and Judy took bites and chewed slowly, staring at the table. Faith broke the silence: "Grandpa came from Boston, didn't he?"

Judy leaned over to pat the girl's hand. "Yes, dear, he did."

"He owned a coffee shop, like Daddy does," Faith continued.

"A bakery, at the beginning, dear."

"Why did we come to Indiana?"

Judy withdrew her hand, and Maddie saw it tremble. Instead of her, Logan answered: "It seems like everyone in American history who wanted to have a better life went west. My father did, when he was very young, and we've been in Indiana ever since."

That satisfied Faith, who went back to eating, so Logan turned to Maddie. "So, you work at an office in Boston? What do you do?"

"I'm an attorney." Maddie hated this. It would be so easy to tell the truth, let it all out, and let the chips fall where they may. "Ordinarily I practice family law. This is something of a sideline, for me." All true, but too much held back. Maddie set her silverware aside, appetite lost.

"An attorney," Logan repeated, with a look toward the ceiling. Maddie realized he must be mentally replaying their earlier conversations, in which she never actually mentioned her job title. "But you told me ..." He paused again, and a wrinkle appeared between his eyebrows.

"I did say my area of expertise is the family," she said, increasingly desperate.

"And its relation to the community, yes. You're in a law firm?"

"Yes." She held her breath.

Leaning forward, Logan pinned her with a narrow eyed gaze. "How long has this firm been in operation?"

That question she didn't expect. "I couldn't say—I've been with the firm five years myself, but there are people there a good deal older than me."

"And one can't be held responsible for the sins of others, of course." Judy shot her son another look.

"Of course not." He sat back, face softening into a smile. "But I guess you're used to the third degree, councilor."

"Well, I don't get into court often." Maddie relaxed. Of course they'd be curious about someone who came into their lives so suddenly, and finding out both sides had a Boston connection must have been as much of a surprise to them as to her.

A few minutes later, as Logan began to ask another question about Maddie's job, Judy glanced at the wall clock. "Oh, dear." She stood, almost knocking over a glass in her haste. "I completely forgot my meeting tonight."

"Meeting?" Logan appeared confused, and the kids even more so. "What meeting?"

"The club." Judy removed her apron and draped it over her chair. "Now, don't worry about the dishes, I'll clean up when I return."

"What club?" Logan asked.

Judy paused in her headlong flight. "The bridge club."

Logan tilted his head. "You don't belong to a bridge club."

"We're starting one. After all, I can't hang around your house all the time, can I?"

She made it sound so accusing, Logan backed down. "Oh—no, of course not. You go ahead and have fun, we'll get the food put away—"

"Fine, but leave the rest of the cleaning up for me. It was wonderful to meet you, Maddie." With that, Judy disappeared.

"What's bridge?" Conner asked.

"It's a card game," Faith explained. "Like Old Maid, or poker. Except I didn't know Grandma played cards."

"Neither did I," Logan mused. "But we should all be willing to try new things, shouldn't we?"

"Like riding a bike," Conner suggested.

"Or roller blading," Faith added.

"Or visiting Indiana," Maddie put in, making the kids giggle. "Now, if everyone's finished, let's put the food away. It would be a shame to waste any of this."

Logan smiled at her, apparently without realizing how adroitly his mother had turned the conversation away from Maddie's profession.

Faith stood beside Conner and declared, "We can get ourselves to bed tonight."

Logan stared at his kids from his seat on the front porch swing. "You can?" Beside him, Maddie looked up from one of Conner's drawings and frowned.

Both the children, who had returned after disappearing into the house for a few minutes, nodded. In fact, Logan realized, they'd been particularly agreeable all day, not fighting with each other once. Now they wanted to skip the regular routine in which Logan helped Conner with his bath, read to them, and tucked them into bed. Should he take their temperatures, or just consider himself lucky?

He turned to Maddie, who sat with an ankle crossed over the other, one hand cupping her chin and the other draped across the seat cushion, regarding the kids with a half-smile. A mild breeze rustled the folds of her dress and fanned her hair across her face, and she looked as relaxed as he'd yet seen her. Relaxed, and so lovely it made his chest ache.

So the kids volunteered to get themselves to bed, this one time. If they wanted to play matchmaker, why should he argue? "Go ahead," he told them, "but no arguments, no water fights, and no wedgies." He addressed Faith alone and added, "And no ghost stories to terrorize your brother."

She rolled her eyes and hugged her father. "I'll read him *Cloudy With a Chance of Meatballs*."

Faith and Conner also hugged Maddie, who returned the gesture rather stiffly, then said their good nights and disappeared into the house. For a moment Logan and Maddie sat side by side in silence, watching the trees and bushes turn warm colors along with the sky. The last few rays of light brushed against the white picket fence along the front of the property, and it took on a glow.

"So, your mother lives with you?" Maddie asked.

"Ever since my wife died. I was going to hire a nanny, but she'd have none of that. Actually, I turned the spare bedroom and second bathroom into an apartment for her." He chuckled at the memory. "Mom said that would keep me from getting a reputation as a man who still lives at home, but she's the one who moved in with me, not the other way around."

"How did—"

"Breast cancer." He'd expected the question, but pushing the answer out still tore at his heart. "No one would have expected ... at that age ..."

Maddie obviously caught his tone—it would have been hard not

65

to. She remained silent for a long, heavy moment. "Volunteering to get themselves to bed—I'm no expert with children, but I take it that was unusual?"

Logan silently thanked her. There was a lot she didn't know about what they went through then, but she didn't ask, and didn't spout any of those endless, empty platitudes that he was thoroughly sick of.

He paused to wave as a neighbor walked by, an elderly man who did a double take and almost veered off the sidewalk at the sight of a woman on the Chandler porch. "Maybe they've decided to become more self-sufficient. You know how kids are at this age, changing every day."

"I don't."

"I'm sorry?" He turned to see a troubled look come over her.

"I don't know what children are like at this age." She ran her fingers over the links of the swing's chain, and Logan could almost feel her right arm, a fraction of an inch from his back. "I don't know children at all."

"At all? But surely you have family—"

"No, not close. No nieces or nephews, no family reunions."

"Company picnics?" Logan couldn't picture an office of stuffy lawyers playing softball and drinking beer. Apparently Maddie couldn't either, because she laughed and turned to him.

"I rarely see my coworkers' family members, and I don't think I want to. They're probably all—" She sobered. "Like me."

"You're not so terrible."

Now Maddie's hand reached forward, to brush his shoulder. "But this isn't the real me. Or ..." She paused, brow furrowed. "Or at least, not the person I've made myself into. That's why I dressed up tonight: To be more of the person I'm used to, aloof and cool and stylish, and not ready to be swept up in the energy of a family like this."

"Why not?"

Her eyes darkened, and she drew away. "Because I've put so much time and energy into my career, it would be a waste to throw it all away. It's not easy being a female lawyer, especially where I come from. I need to focus, and work long hours, and sacrifice, and ... all that."

"You sound like you're trying to convince yourself." He reached out to and found her hand warm and damp, as if she were nervous. *Well, that made two of them.* "Maybe you need a little time off, to think of something other than work."

With her other hand she covered his, and met his gaze squarely. "If I—if we get involved ... we'll both get hurt. I guarantee it."

"If there's one thing life has taught me, it's that there are no guarantees." She swallowed, and Logan followed her throat up to her lips. "Well, there is one ..."

"What?"

"I guarantee I'm going to kiss you."

Maddie's breath caught and her eyes widened, as if in panic. Not the reaction he'd hoped for, but she also leaned forward a bit. "That's a terrible idea."

"Not from where I'm sitting." Everything for the last two days seemed to lead to this, as he cupped Maddie's chin, tipped her head back, and pressed his lips to hers.

Heaven—warm and soft and alive, all he could imagine. Also very, very brief.

Before Logan was fully aware of what happened, Maddie jerked away and stumbled to her feet, almost tipping him out of the swing. She braced herself on the porch rail, poised to run, her face masked in panic, but her words were the last he expected:

"Someone fell."

Logan stared up at her, unable to comprehend until he heard Faith's shout through the screen door, from the top of the stairs: "Dad, I heard Conner fall in the bathtub!"

She sounded more annoyed than upset, but Logan jumped out of the swing to make sure his son didn't break a tooth or suffer a bump on the head. He took one step before Maddie jerked the door open, dashing into the house at full speed.

Logan glimpsed sheer terror on her face, the kind of fright he couldn't imagine in his worst nightmare. As he tried to catch up with her, he realized only having her own nightmare come true could explain the extreme reaction.

Maddie pounded up the stairs, past a startled Faith, who looked on in confusion as her father moved past her. By the time Logan reached the bathroom Maddie knelt on the floor and held a soaked Conner, who was wrapped in a bath towel, in her arms.

Conner coughed violently, but Logan saw no sign of injury. That didn't stop Maddie, who ran one hand over the boy in a search for broken bones while she slapped his back with another. "Call 911!" she ordered Logan. "Get an ambulance!"

Conner tried to speak, but between the coughs and the back slaps couldn't get anything out.

"Wait a minute—" Logan began, reaching down to them.

Maddie slapped his hand away. "Damn it, he needs to be in the hospital! Faith, call 911!"

From the doorway Faith looked to her father, who shook his head. Maddie swept Conner into her arms and stood, almost knocking down both Logan and Faith as she tried to get through the door. When Logan took her arm she jerked it away. "He could have drowned," she insisted.

"I'm okay," Conner said, his voice raspy but strong. "I just slipped."

Stopped in her tracks, Maddie stared down at the boy, then at Faith, who looked terrified. "Well—you shouldn't let him take a bath by himself, Logan! Don't you see what almost happened?"

"Faith was right outside the door, and there's not a foot of water in the tub—"

"It doesn't take one inch!"

"Maddie, let me down," Conner begged. She gazed at him again, then settled him onto the floor and, chest heaving, slipped past Faith into the hallway.

For a moment the Chandler family stood silently, while Logan wondered if his kids were as surprised at Maddie's reaction as he was. Then he heard a noise from the hallway, something that sounded very much like a sob.

Faith poked her head through the doorway, then turned back to whisper, "Daddy, Maddie's crying."

"I'm sorry." Conner looked ready to cry himself.

"It's not your fault." He gave his son a much gentler pat on the back, and asked Faith to help clean up the mess before stepping into the hallway.

Maddie stood at the top of the stairway, hands over her face. Water soaked the front of her rainbow colored dress, and strands of hair had loosened from her careful hairstyle to halo around her cheeks.

"Maddie." From behind, he put his arms around her waist. She fell back against him.

"I'm sorry." She'd regained control of her voice and moved away from him, but her entire body shook.

"You really don't have much experience with kids, huh?"

"That's not it." She turned to show red rimmed eyes and tear streaks down her cheeks. "My sister."

"Your—"

"She died. Drowned. She was Conner's age." Her voice broke again.

Logan felt something in him break, too. He reached forward, but she stepped back to avoid his touch. "Don't. Don't feel sorry for me. I could have saved her."

Then she turned, stumbled down the stairs, and slammed through the front door before Logan could catch his breath. For a long time he stood, staring at the doorway, unable to move or believe.

# CHAPTER FIVE

Maddie wasn't surprised when someone knocked on her door at 8 o'clock the next morning. The remarkable part was that it took him so long to track her down.

She cinched her peach sherpa robe and headed toward the door, all too aware that she wore no makeup, and had tied her hair back in a tight ponytail. Going glamorous hadn't phased him a bit, so maybe transforming into a plain working woman would turn him off. The dark bags under her eyes could only help.

She kicked aside a second ruined pair of pantyhose, torn at some point during her panic attack at Logan's house. They looked like she felt.

Bracing herself for a reaction, Maddie opened the door and saw Logan, dressed in blue jeans and a dark polo shirt, holding a paper bag. "Good morning!" he said, as cheerful as if she'd never dropped that bombshell on him the previous night.

"How did you find me?" She tried to sound listless, but the life in his eyes—and muscles under his cotton shirt—combined to send her heart on a lap around the Indianapolis Motor Speedway. Heaven help her, she was happy to see him.

"There are three places to stay in town, and this is the ritziest of them. Then I thought 'suite', and the rest was a matter of knocking on doors until you opened one." He shook the bag. "I thought you'd need breakfast."

"After what your mother stuffed into me?" But she stood aside, then closed the door behind him.

Logan pulled out rolls, juice, and covered bowls of fruit, setting them out on a small table in the outer room. "You're looking better than I thought you would."

Better? She could only imagine what he'd expected.

"Coffee?" He held up a familiar looking thermos.

"Flavor?"

"Black."

"Pour."

"Done." Logan filled two cups, and passed one to her. "There's more where that came from—an entire forest full of beans with your name on them."

When she didn't answer he glanced up, and she saw the concern in his eyes. "I assume you didn't sleep well last night."

"True." With a sigh, she settled into a chair opposite him, and took a long sip of java. "It hasn't been a good week."

"How could that be?" He grinned. "You met us, after all."

"Didn't you hear what I told you last night?" Maddie didn't mean it to come out so sharply, but Logan just shrugged.

"I thought you'd like to tell me the rest of the story."

"What makes you think there's a rest of the story?"

"As you lawyers might say, it was a supposition. Open wide." He held out a chunk of watermelon, and without thinking she ate it. "Do you want to start now, or wait until after breakfast?"

"You're extremely presumptuous." As he started to pop an orange slice into his mouth, she grabbed it away and ate it herself. Usually she went into a three day funk whenever memories of her sister's death were dredged up, but his ceaseless upbeat mood kept chasing her blues away. She already felt improved enough to tease him.

"If you're saying I don't have the right to ask—"

Maddie reached forward again, to put a finger over his mouth. "I'm not saying that." She picked up a roll, and counted silently to five while studying it. "I'm just saying I'm going to make you wait." Then, slowly, she ate the roll while Logan sat back and watched her, his lips quirked upward.

Maddie realized with a start that, despite those old wounds torn open the night before, she was enjoying this. She used a similar technique in the courtroom: Let the witness, or the other attorney, stew for a bit until they got upset and started saying things they shouldn't. Did she like torturing people, or was it the fact that Logan saw through her tricks that gave her a light feeling despite the topic of conversation? In any case, she couldn't avoid it forever, so she wiped her lips, picked up the knife he'd set out to slice the fruit, and brandished it between them.

"Suppose I lived with you, and helped watch Conner sometimes."

"I wouldn't hesitate to let you."

She paused, thrown by his trust, but quickly recovered. "Suppose I didn't stop him from playing with this knife, and while running with it he fell and stabbed himself. Would I not be responsible?"

Now Logan frowned, affected by her personalized story, as she knew he would be. "Legally, or morally?"

"Would you care about the difference?"

"No. And yes, I suppose you would be responsible, if you gave him the knife."

"My sister was six years old. She drowned in my family's swimming pool." Maddie dropped the knife, surprised that her voice shook only a little.

Logan rubbed his chin and examined the knife for a moment, then looked her into the eyes. "That's not the whole story."

"What?"

"Did you tell her to go swim in the pool?"

"No, of course not—she couldn't swim."

He nodded. "And where were you two supposed to be?"

"I was gone, to my friend's house—" Her throat constricted as it played through her mind, the way it always did the few times she'd tried to tell the story. "I wasn't supposed to go. I snuck out …" She could still remember the horror, and the self-loathing when she arrived home to find the police, the ambulance—the coroner. The only other reaction she'd ever had was anger at her fiancé when she finally brought herself to tell him—and he dismissively told her to get over it.

"You weren't even there?"

Maddie glared at him. Those had been the first words out of her fiancé's mouth. "I was supposed to be there!"

Logan leaned forward. "Who *was* there?"

"Our guardians, the staff …"

He started to speak, then stopped as if rethinking what he should say. "If anything it was a sin of omission, not commission."

She stared at him, while he carefully bit down on a slice of apple, and she recognized her own technique being used against her.

"Your knife example?" He held up another apple slice. "Apples and oranges. You didn't encourage her to play in the pool, therefore you aren't guilty of what you think you are. Your example should have been leaving Conner in someone else's care, and not knowing when he took the knife himself."

Maddie opened her mouth to speak, but nothing came out.

"How old were you?"

She took a shuddering breath. "Twelve."

"You're beating yourself up for something that happened when you were twelve, and you weren't even there?" Logan took Maddie's hands, and fixed her with an intense stare. "And you've been avoiding children ever since? Maddie, it was a tragedy, but also an accident—and you've served a long enough sentence. Give yourself time served, and walk away."

She felt a tear roll down her cheek, but couldn't express how she felt in words. Instead she asked, "Did you ever consider becoming a lawyer?"

"And wear a suit every day?" He used a finger to wipe her tear away. "Actually, I was prelaw, but I ended up following in my father's footsteps and getting a business degree. It seemed more honest."

Although she knew he was joking, the last comment jolted Maddie. "I've been meaning to talk to you on that subject—"

"Later. I never got a chance to finish that kiss." Logan leaned forward across the table and touched his lips to hers. She stiffened, intent on telling him the truth about her presence, then gave up and parted her lips as her senses melted into him. He half stood, one hand on her neck to draw her closer, and she decided his kiss was the most persuasive argument ever made.

Someone banged hard on the hotel room door.

With a groan, Logan broke contact and fell back into his chair. "It's the kiss police."

"They must be here to give you a medal." Trying to hide her disappointment, Maddie got up and hurried toward the door, then paused to call back, "A Purple Lip, maybe?" She saw him give a wicked grin, then turned back as the intruder knocked again.

If this was a hotel employee, they could forget about a tip. Swinging open the door, she prepared to shoo the visitor away.

A waifish figure, half a head shorter than Maddie, stood poised to knock once more. Her hair, black as a moonless night, dove in a straight line to the small of her back, while dark skin, large brown eyes, and high cheekbones finished the story of her ancestry.

Maddie turned back to Logan. "The natives are restless." He rose, looking surprised at her politically incorrect words.

"Is that nice?" The girl marched into the room and gazed around, as if measuring every corner. "I drove all night to get here." She wore an off white peasant skirt and a matching blouse, with the only adornment a leather pouch tied to her belt. Overall she could pass for a 60s hippie.

But Maddie knew better. Taking the other woman's arm, she swung her around to face an approaching Logan. "Dena Hantaywee, this is Logan Chandler."

Looking uninterested, Dena reached out her hand. "Charmed." But as soon as their fingers touched, she jumped and looked him up and down with fresh interest. "Wow! *You* are surrounded by spirits." Releasing her grip, she circled him once, then marched back toward the door.

"You," Logan whispered to Maddie, "have interesting friends."

She couldn't argue that. "You probably expected I'd surround myself with Boston socialites named Heather and Buffy."

At the door Dena gestured with a crooked finger, then moved aside. Two men in overalls marched with purpose into the room, depositing boxes and cases according to Dena's terse directions. They moved aside the remains of breakfast to make room for a new, larger table, and deposited a file cabinet next to it. Within minutes, they'd loaded the table with a laptop, printer/copier, and a store full of office supplies.

When the workers left, Logan came out of the bedroom doorway—where he'd taken refuge to keep from being run over—and watched Dena fire up the laptop. "I'm ... impressed. But you need a coffee maker."

"It's temporary, while we arrange some office space." Dena switched the computer on and listened for the startup chime before settling into a chair. "I, for one, need better seating."

Logan looked around again and scratched the back of his neck. "And this is all for research?"

Maddie felt the cold grip of panic clutch her spine.

"Oh, sure." Dena nodded, then reached behind her into the kitchenette, to steal a piece of fruit. "You've got to have your facts in order and your arguments prepared, that's what Maddie teaches." She gave Logan still another appraisal. "So, are you here to fight the good fight? With no more support than this from the powers that be, we could use all the help we could get."

Logan took his own turn with the appraising stare, but before he could speak Maddie hustled forward.

"I'd hardly call research a fight—you just find out what people want and how they feel, no fighting involved. Wouldn't you say?" Standing between the other two, she gave Dena a pleading look.

"No." Dena shook her head. "I mean, yes. I misspoke."

"Oh." Although still looking puzzled, Logan seemed to accept Maddie's latest half-truth, especially when Dena quickly changed the subject by holding up a set of car keys.

"You made a huge mistake, young lady—you gave me these."

Maddie immediately brightened. "My Porsche? You brought my Porsche?"

"Yeah, and it'll do triple digits on the toll road."

Maddie impulsively hugged her friend, then held her out at arm's length. "Did you—"

"Washed and waxed," Dena said with a grin. "And no, I didn't get crumbs on the leather seats. Or at least, if I did you'll never know."

Maddie sighed in true car-lover contentment.

"That's just how I look when I get that first cup of hot java in the morning," Logan told her.

"Well, she was the first luxury I ever bought for myself." Seeing Logan's questioning look, Maddie added, "The Porsche, I mean, not Dena."

"I'm not a luxury," Dena explained, "I'm job related. In fact, I think Maddie deducts me from her taxes."

"Makes business sense," Logan said. "I suppose I should leave you two to get organized, then."

Maddie nodded, both disappointed and relieved. "It's going to be hectic around here for a bit." She lightly kissed him on the cheek, a far cry from the heat they'd experienced earlier. "Tell the kids I said hello."

"Tell them yourself, Friday night."

"I'm sorry?"

"Two new movies at the drive-in Friday. They—the kids, not the movies—respectfully requested your appearance, which is another way of saying they won't take no for an answer."

"But—I—"

"Surely your partner will give you Friday night off? That gives you two days to get … organized. And this time I promise not to spill your popcorn, let alone tackle you." He turned an expectant gaze on Dena.

The other woman looked from one to the other, then got up to raid the fruit bowls again. Maddie could tell she was being deliberately casual. "Actually, I'm her assistant, so I can't tell her what to do. Besides, even lawyers should take Friday night off."

"Then it's a date. I'll pick you up early, we don't want to lose our place on a busy night." With a wave Logan stepped out, closing the door behind him.

For a moment the two women stood in silence. Then Dena waved an accusatory banana at her boss. "Babe, you've been holding out. You have a lot to explain."

*Yes—to everyone.* Maddie sank into the other chair and held her head in her hands. "I've been bad."

"Then why did he still have clothes on?"

"That's not what I meant!" But Dena's comment reminded her she still needed to prepare for the day, so Maddie got up and plodded into the bedroom. As she opened a suitcase and poked through it, Dena followed and perched on a corner of the bed. She punched the mattress.

"Good thing you got a double, roomie."

"What?"

"I couldn't find a room anywhere. Something about Jay Leno and a car show."

"Fine." Maddie couldn't remember ever sharing a bed as an adult, although the thought of sharing one with Logan occurred to her earlier—which meant having Dena here was for the best. "I don't suppose you brought some Sheer Invites?"

"Babe, I'm full of sheer invites." Dena shook her head. "You mean those ironclad pantyhose? You shouldn't need more—you couldn't put a run in those things with a chain saw."

"Never mind. Just please tell me you don't sleep in the nude."

Dena looked surprised. "Is there another way?"

"Try this." Maddie pulled off her robe to reveal her favorite nightgown, white satin that came to mid-thigh. "I realize your parents are free spirits, but surely they've heard of nightwear."

"If you'd taken your robe off ten minutes ago, Logan Chandler would have pushed me out the door and I'd be cooling my heels in the hallway. Do you really think walking around in that is less suggestive than going natural?"

"Maybe not, but for me sleeping with a nude woman is … creepy. Well, out of the ordinary. For me." Maddie shrugged out of the nightgown and made for the shower.

Behind her Dena called, "Okay, so I'll wear a T-shirt—you know I once had to share a bed with two other girls at the shelter. Leave the bathroom door open, so we can talk."

"Why? What's going on at the office?" Maddie stepped into the shower stall, letting the warm water wash over her.

"Forget the office—I just heard you use the word 'creepy'. That is *not* you. And when I got here you had a man in your room but hadn't done your hair or makeup. It's like the evil lawyer you is gone, replaced by your normal twin sister."

Maddie loosened her hair and scrubbed shampoo into it, all the while wondering if she could change that much in two short days. It was the worst possible thing that could happen. She needed that hard, clear thinking lawyer back, or she'd lose her grip on this development case, and her career.

"So?" Judging from Dena's voice, she now stood in the bathroom doorway.

"So what?"

"Are you loosening up in your old age? You're what—twenty-nine? What about the guy? What's all this business about being tackled, and kids, and a date Friday night?"

"Do you see the loofah?" As she spoke the words a black loofah came sailing over the shower wall. Maddie still didn't know how Dena sensed what she needed before it was called for, but she appreciated her assistant's ability—although she'd never needed it in the shower before.

"Heaven forbid you should cleanse your precious body with a lowly washcloth. Now, start talking or I'll flush the toilet."

"I met him at the drive-in."

That brought a pause so long Maddie began rinsing off before Dena spoke again. "You went to a drive-in?"

"The drive-in is why we're here. I need to do my research, don't I?"

"Well ... sure." Dena giggled. "I'm picturing you sitting in a van with a tub of popcorn and a soda." She took on a haughty tone: "With which fork does one eat popcorn? Where's the valet? Please inform the concierge that a person of Boston society does not park her own car. What? No after-feature wine?"

As she shut off the water Maddie chuckled despite herself, then jumped when a bath towel came sailing over the wall. "Thank you."

"I live to serve," Dena called. "Actually, I live to hear good, juicy stories. So spill."

With a sigh, Maddie described the movie night and the following day, including the bathroom mishap that led Maddie to tell the story of her sister's death. After wrapping the towel around her she emerged into the bedroom, where she found Dena rummaging through Maddie's suitcases.

"You are so running out of clothes," Dena announced, while she laid a rather conservative blue dress out on the bed.

"Some are at the dry cleaners, and one I tossed into a trash bin out back. But I have plenty of clean underwear—."

"Cause momma always said ..." they finished together.

Rolling her eyes, Dena reached into another bag and tossed her a bra and panties. "Wear just this to the hearings, so you'll have at least half the population on your side. But you also need something for the drive-in—do you even own blue jeans?"

"No."

"We need to do some major shopping, and not at Saks. Get your card out and prepare to see it smoke."

"Fine, but I won't need jeans—I'm not going to the drive-in." Maddie had made that decision in the shower, while thinking about the way her actions and speech changed since she reached Indiana. And the way she'd fallen so fast for the kind of man she'd never looked twice at before.

"Why not?"

Shucking the towel, Maddie pulled on underwear and considered the question. "It isn't necessary to the job."

"The job? But you could spend more time getting a feel for the place, and also maybe spend some time getting a feel of that gorgeous hunk of Hoosier grown beefcake!"

She held the dress out, but Maddie refused it. "Ladies wear slips," Maddie reminded her assistant. She dug one out of her underwear case, along with the third pair of Sheer Invites.

"I don't own one, but I've got you beat by six jeans. Now, answer the question, counselor."

"Fine! I've already got a feel for the drive-in, it doesn't take that much. And Logan Chandler is leading the opposition to the new airport."

Maddie finished dressing in silence.

When she started doing her hair Dena slapped her hands away, led her to a seat on the bed, and went to work with brush and curling iron. "A lady should have her hair done, not do it herself."

"You'll get no raise for this."

But Dena's joking mood had vanished. "This is just the type of thing the partners do: make friends with the opponents, then grill them for information. You've learned a lot from them." An agitated swipe of the brush almost pulled Maddie off the chair. "You've also learned what not to do, from one partner in particular. Or have you forgotten that mixing business with pleasure is what got you here to begin with?"

"I've forgotten nothing."

"Then honey, you'd better stick strictly to business, or hang up the whole thing and go for the pleasure."

"I—"

"Look, if you get fired, I get fired. I know you've never experienced the joy of welfare and the unemployment line, but it's not nearly the all-day party it's cracked up to be."

Maddie sat in silence, while Dena finished her hair. Then she stood up, marched to the phone, and dialed a number she'd memorized the day before.

"Chandler residence."

"Hi, Faith, this is Maddie." Maddie had hoped Logan's mother, or Logan himself, would answer the phone. It would make what she must do much easier.

"Maddie! Conner, it's Maddie!" Maddie winced as the boy screeched in the background.

"Um, Faith, I have some bad news. I'm afraid I'm not going to be able to go with you to the drive-in Friday."

"Oh, no." Faith's disappointment hit Maddie with an almost physical force. "You can't say no. We counted on you to come with us." In the background, Conner loudly protested.

"I know, but something very important came up—"

"We're making special snacks for you, and we're bringing lawn chairs so everybody can see the movie and a radio and extra blankets and everything."

"That sounds lovely—"

"I drew you some more pictures!" Conner yelled into the phone, and for a moment Maddie heard a struggle that turned out to be Faith grabbing the phone back from her brother.

"He's also got his favorite toys to show you. And I'm bringing this necklace, my mommy gave it to me, and we got the van cleaned and—"

"But, Faith—" Maddie noticed Dena move in to hear both sides of the conversation. She looked gleeful to see her boss lose an argument for once, especially to a child. "My assistant just arrived from Boston, and we need to have meetings and do some work—"

"Not on a Friday night!"

"No—of course not. But Dena's never been to Indiana, and has no friends, and she'd be all alone if I didn't stay with her."

Laughing silently, Dena dropped onto the bed and pantomimed stripping her clothes off. Maddie looked around to throw something at her, but Faith's next words distracted her:

"Then bring your assistant with you. I bet she likes movies."

Maddie looked at Dena. For a moment Dena, who pretended to snore and kick an imaginary Maddie off the bed, didn't notice. Then the other woman glimpsed her boss' expression, and sat up. "What?"

"You know something, Faith? I believe that might just be a marvelous idea."

Dena dashed back to the phone and tried to listen in. "What's a marvelous idea?" But she heard only two children cheering.

After Maddie said good-bye and hung up, she turned back to Dena with a look that made the other woman take a step backward. "You asked for it, young lady."

"What? Asked for what?"

"We're both going to the drive-in."

"We—" Frowning, Dena shook her head. "What's that supposed to accomplish?"

"You're right that we both need to be more familiar with the situation. More important, I didn't disappoint the children, and with you along there's no chance I'll be left alone with Logan Chandler."

"Ah—now you're thinking like a lawyer." Dena considered the idea for a moment. "So, do you think there's a chance I'll be left alone with him?"

"Don't make me pull your benefits." She lightly slapped her friend on the back of the head, then turned to start the day's work. But for the rest of the day her thoughts kept blurring into Friday night, and she couldn't get over the feeling this plan could all too easily backfire.

# CHAPTER SIX

Maddie stood by Logan's van, in the same spot where he'd parked the night they met. She looked around as cars, trucks and vans took the prime spots in the middle of the lot, while a line of vehicles stretched out along the highway, waiting their turn to get in. The sun still stood in the western sky, at least half an hour from setting. It seemed everyone in Indiana wanted to come see the new Disney movie, and a flick about a comic book character come to life.

At the base of the big silver screen, a dozen children roamed the little playground while their parents set up blankets, lawn chairs, and citronella candles to drive away bugs. Maddie saw no insects, but assumed they had all flown off to find whoever was grilling hot dogs and hamburgers—against the posted rules—somewhere on the other end of the lot.

"Incredible." She watched a pickup truck load of teenagers back into a place nearby. Almost before they came to a stop the passengers leaped out like a racing team, to set up what amounted to a tailgate party.

"What's incredible?" Dena passed her with a lawn chair, which she unfolded right in front of the van's hood. With every nearby space filled, there was no room to place them beside the vehicle.

"Two thirds of these people have bumper stickers to save the drive-in."

"And all of them know Logan." Dena gave her boss a pointed look, then walked around her to retrieve another lawn chair. "Hey, brats, have you got the radio?"

"Yeah!" Conner yelled. He hopped out of the van, clutching a portable radio, while Faith followed with a small cooler. Maddie almost cried out when they raced forward, but the children stuck close to the side of the van and avoided both the car beside them and the passing traffic in front, like the drive-in veterans they were.

"Well, make sure the batteries are good." Grabbing a third chair, Dena set it up in line with the other two.

"Wait a minute." Maddie grabbed Dena by the arm and pointed to the folding chairs. "Why three?"

"So I can sit with the kids, of course. You're the one so worried about their welfare." She attempted an innocent smile.

"Yes, but—"

"Dena's sitting with us!" Conner yelled.

"In the middle," Faith confirmed, "so she has to make Conner be quiet."

"But—"

Before she could protest further, Maddie heard Logan's voice behind her: "Another argument over seating arrangements?"

She turned to see him holding two tubs of popcorn and a bottle of water, which, with some difficulty, he held out to her. "From Tupper."

Perrier. The brand didn't seem so important to her anymore, but it gave her hope that Tupper wasn't so scatterbrained, after all. "Thank you."

"And popcorn for the outdoor crew." He held a tub out toward Dena, but she shook her head.

"Can you keep it in the van? The kids and I are going to the playground."

"You what?" Maddie stared at her, but Logan turned to stow the popcorn without comment, as if he'd expected it.

"We've got a ticket to slide, woman. And swing." Dena held up two colorful plastic disks. "Plus, it's high time these children learned the fine art of Frisbee hot dogging. We'll be back for the coming attractions." Leaning closer to Maddie, she whispered, "And that'll leave you time to work through your already-here attractions." Then the three, holding hands and watching for cross traffic, set off to go play.

"Incredible."

Logan moved the radio and cooler to the ground beneath the center chair. Straightening, he regarded her with a raised eyebrow. "Incredible?"

"Dena. I've never seen her interact with children, but I shouldn't be surprised they took to her so quickly." What did surprise her was the wistful tone she heard in her own voice.

Logan must have heard it too, because he laid a hand on her shoulder and kissed the top of her head. "They see her as a buddy, but to them you're more of a princess."

"Unapproachable."

"Beautiful."

"But I'm a lawyer. Obnoxious, suspected, and unpopular." When she caught his puzzled look, Maddie explained, "It's how John Adams once described himself. I consider him something of a personal hero, a role model."

"You consider an obnoxious, unpopular guy who died two hundred years ago to be your hero—I'll try not to be too jealous. He was from Massachusetts, wasn't he? Same as you. But why would you want to take after someone who thought of himself that way?"

"Because he also said, 'Facts are stubborn things; and whatever may be our wishes, our inclinations, or the dictates of our passion, they cannot alter the state of facts and evidence'. That's my favorite quote."

Logan regarded her silently, eyes narrow. "I don't think I like that quote. Facts are all well and good in a courtroom, but it sounds like he's trying to deny the power of wishes, and passion. What's life with only facts?"

"Easier," Maddie whispered. "Pursuing just the facts got me through some difficult times." Lonely times, before she met Dena … and often afterward.

Instead of arguing, Logan lightly rubbed her arm, transferring his warmth to her. "Well, maybe Dena can play because she didn't have any childhood traumas to worry about."

"Actually, she did. Her family went bankrupt, and they were thrown out onto the streets when she was a teenager." Maddie could see Dena in the distance, tossing the bright disks to the children and clowning around, not the least bit concerned that she frolicked in front of hundreds of occupied cars. "Dena says her parents taught her to treat life as an adventure, something to be savored even when everything's going wrong. She lost her fiancé a few years ago, but … I sometimes call her 'The Undefeatable Dena", because she always bounces back."

But Dena did go through some very difficult times, and as Maddie thought back on it, she couldn't remember ever seeing her friend this happy. If Maddie'd had the support of a close family, could she have handled her own tragedy differently?

For a moment they watched the three play, then Logan brought her back to the present by gesturing behind them. "Let's sit."

At least they weren't in the back, Maddie thought, as Logan took his seat and tilted the steering wheel out of the way. Grinning, he gestured down at the familiar thermos, now positioned between their seats. "Would you like a chaser with that water?"

"You first."

He poured himself a cup, and took a cautious sip. For a long moment, head cocked, he stared off into the distance. Then he carefully poured the remaining coffee back into the thermos. "Seemed like a good idea at the time. After all, most people who like coffee also like butter on their toast, right?"

Maddie couldn't help laughing. "Would that be the same people who pour decaf over their pancakes?"

She watched his profile while he tuned the radio, and saw a strong chin, a thatch of thick sandy hair across his forehead, alert eyes which revealed a hint of lines when he smiled. His hands were large and strong, perfect for kneading tight muscles or making love.

With his right hand he reached out, took her left, and held it. She took a sip of water, to rinse her dry mouth.

Just as Maddie braced herself to ask what he was thinking, Logan spoke: "I like your outfit."

It seemed his thoughts paralleled hers. "Dena picked it out." Actually, Dena tried to force her into jeans, but they'd settled on white slacks and a yellow tank top, and sandals. Maddie briefly considered shorts, and realized she never wore them in public except at the gym. Logan did wear jeans, along with a polo shirt the same color, coincidentally, as her top.

After another short silence, Logan spoke again. "I can't believe you'd never been to the drive-in."

"My childhood must have been a bit different from yours." Her voice caught, and she took another drink of water.

"Could be." He squeezed her hand. "Let's compare. You already know my history with the drive-in."

"I know it, but I'm not sure I get it."

"I suppose it's funny to a big city girl like you, but this was the center of my social life. I like to point out—maybe too often—that my first job was here, and my first date. My wife and I seriously considered getting married here, until her mother talked some sense into us."

Maddie smiled at the thought. "I never would have imagined it, but it would fit you. Did you honeymoon in a camper on the back row?"

"I'm not that much of a diehard. But we were here when she went into labor with Faith—we missed the double feature that night." He turned in his seat to more directly face her. "Now, your turn: I take it your social life didn't involve sitting in a car at the movies?"

Fair enough. "Just after my sister was born, my mother and father died in a plane crash. I wasn't raised by parents; I was raised by a trust fund. Strict. Sterile. Piano and voice tutors, lessons in the social graces, the best Catholic girl's school—"

"Really?" Logan winked. "Still got the outfit?"

"Don't start. We had an associate who wouldn't leave the whole Catholic schoolgirl thing alone, and I had to register a formal complaint. He works for legal aid now."

"I stand politically corrected." He looked toward the screen for a moment, then turned back with a leer. "Still, at the risk of being sued—"

"In my closet at home. And yes, it still fits." Maddie assumed—and half hoped—he'd follow that up with a suggestive comment, but instead Logan seemed lost in thought for a moment.

"You don't strike me as the type who'd keep something around once it's not needed any more. Why keep a school uniform you haven't worn in a decade?"

Wow. What a good question. "Well ... I suppose it was because my guardians didn't let me keep many personal belongings, and so the uniform was one of the few things left over from my childhood."

"Hm." Logan released her hand, leaned back in his seat and stared at the van's ceiling.

"I feel like I'm being analyzed."

"No, I'm just picturing you in the outfit." He grinned, then had to fend her off when she slapped at him. "Kidding!" He grabbed her wrists, and before she knew it leaned in to touch their lips together.

The contact, far too short, left her lips burning for more. She reached for the water bottle again, trying to cool down, while he popped the tab of a soda can and also took a long drink. The look they exchanged was almost shy. When he broke the silence his words, spoken in a gentle tone, were unexpected.

"So, your apartment is roomy but rather sterile, with a few personal things stowed away in the back of your closet where no one ever sees them. Nice artwork on the walls, expensive furniture and a deluxe stereo system, but no visitors."

It was as if he'd walked through the place. "It's a townhouse, technically," she breathed. "And Dena lived with me for six months after her boyfriend died, until ..."

93

"Until?" He paused in the act of taking a sip, regarding her over the can.

"Until I started dating a man who thought it was inappropriate for a personal assistant to share a home with her boss." Maddie held her breath.

When Logan spoke again he sounded as upset as Maddie feared, but not on the subject she'd anticipated. "You kicked Dena *out?*"

"I found her a nice apartment just down the street."

"Just months after her fiancé died?"

"Look, I rescued her. She lost her job and was being evicted. And I stayed up with her crying all night, more times than you can imagine—"

"There it is." Logan's look of indignation melted into a smile.

"There what is?"

"The human Maddie. Sometimes I get the feeling your lawyer side battles your human side, and the lawyer is winning." He reached out to stroke her cheek. "But the human Maddie gave Dena a safety net when she was about to hit bottom."

Maddie touched his arm, and marveled at his warmth and understanding. She could count on one hand—no, two fingers—the number of people who could see through the wall she'd built around herself. For him, as with Dena, it seemed to come naturally.

"So, tell me about this jerk boyfriend."

With a grimace, she released his hand and looked away. "He's a jerk."

"Could you be more specific?"

"He's a big jerk."

"Bigger than me?" Only then did Maddie realize Logan showed curiosity, more than jealousy.

"No, you could twist him like a pretzel. But of course, if you did that he'd haul you into court, and see to it you lost everything you own to pay his alleged medical expenses, while you rot in jail." As she spoke, Maddie realized the same could be said of any of the partners, or any associate with half a chance to become a partner.

"Sounds like a guy who gets what he wants—so why didn't he get to keep you?"

Maddie blew out a breath and tapped her fingers on the dashboard. "Really, 'he's a jerk' covers it. I'm afraid my lawyer side thought a—partnership—would make sense. We shared similar interests, after all, and when I attended social functions—"

"Bowling night?"

"Company sponsored art shows, opera, dinner parties." Maddie stopped, and realized she hadn't enjoyed a social function for years. "Anyway, he always came, too, and he was charming and flattering, and pretty soon we went to the same functions as a couple. Then, one day, the waiter took the lid off the dessert, to reveal a ring."

"A big ring," Logan prodded.

"Yes. His arguments for a merger seemed so logical ... you know, I never technically said yes, but from that night on he took over my life. I dressed differently, wore my hair differently, kicked Dena out—"

"Into a very nice apartment just down the street," Logan reminded her with a sympathetic smile.

"Then, one day, he told me I had to get rid of 'that girl' as my assistant because she didn't fit the company image, and didn't know her place. I became angry, we argued, I threw a drink in his face—it was all very dramatic." She took a deep breath. "In front of the partners."

"You soaked him in front of the partners?"

"No, not just soaked him. Soaked him and raised a goose bump on his head—and got an olive stuck in his nose."

For a moment Logan stared at her, then his eyes widened. "You threw the glass at him?"

"After I dropped the ring into it. Just a small scar above the hairline, hardly noticeable—"

But Logan held a finger up to stop her. In the fading light she saw him cock his head to one side, then his lips slowly turned up. "So that's it—you're exiled here! I wondered how an upscale Boston attorney ended up in the boondocks—you're being punished with this pointless little research project, aren't you?"

Maddie nodded weakly. "I'm being punished, yes." And the punishment would get worse before it got better. "But maybe it's for the best. Naturally there are bad feelings, and putting some distance between us—"

"But he's a controlling ass. Why isn't he the one being exiled?"

"Oh, Logan." She laid a hand on his thigh, then realized what she was doing and jerked it away. "He's a partner, and law firms are still a man's world. Half the partners, and the associates, probably think I dated him to further my career, anyway. When I threw that drink on him it was the worst possible faux pas. Well, not the worst—Dena's thought of some worse things to do to him, since. But now it's best that I take my medicine, don't make waves, and be thankful we won't see each other again for a long time."

"You'll see him again, soon," Logan said, his voice dark.

"What?"

"An ex-boyfriend in the same company as you? He'll show up when you least expect it, guaranteed. It's Murphy's Law of Romance: The Ex always pops up at the worst possible time, usually when a new romance is brewing." Frowning, he added, "Brace yourself for it."

But Maddie shook her head. "Gil Tremayne would not be caught dead amongst the commoners in rural Indiana. You might as well ask him to go to a five star restaurant and serve his own food."

Hearing the name made Logan smile again. "Gil Tremayne?"

"Gilroy." It had never struck her before, but now his full name sounded hilarious, and they were both still laughing when Dena and the kids returned.

Faith and Conner, out of breath, took their seats immediately, but Dena leaned into the van to retrieve their popcorn. "Having fun?"

"You know it," Logan told her. "Little monsters wearing you out?"

"Absolutely." Framed in the last rays of a setting sun, Dena looked past him to Maddie. "I haven't had this much fun since the last company function my boss dragged me to."

Maddie fixed her with a warning glare. "He knows about the drink."

"The olive—?"

"In the nose," Logan said with a smile.

"Aw. I missed seeing the look on your face." Pouting, Dena walked to the front of the van and sat between the kids, as the sun's disk slipped under trees on the horizon. Minutes later, as the last few cars found places near the rear of the lot, the coming attractions began.

Logan glanced at her, and for a moment she thought he'd kiss her again. But instead he laced his fingers through hers, as if it was the most natural thing in the world. In a way, sitting comfortable next to each other, arms pressed together, was almost as nice as the kiss. Coming attractions, indeed.

Maddie wasn't thrilled by previews of a science fiction thriller, thought an upcoming romantic comedy looked good, and she laughed despite herself at scenes of a talking dog and a comic actor she'd never heard of. Overall it looked like good escapist fare for the summer.

"A pretty good crop coming up," Logan commented, as opening title rolled for the first feature.

"But it doesn't say when they'll play here," Maddie complained, thinking of how difficult it was to plan around meetings and events.

"Sometimes you just have to roll the dice. Over the years I've had a lot of surprises, good and bad. I might be the only person who ever saw 'Waterworld', or the original 'Buffy the Vampire Slayer'."

It seemed even a bad movie was good in this place. Maddie began to see why, and tried to ignore the fact that, if she did her job well, the silver screen would be gone within months. Then the only thing to watch would be airplanes coming in for a landing.

The Disney flick was ... well, cute. With the tickets a third of what she would pay in Boston, she couldn't complain. During intermission Dena and the kids raided the big cooler in the back seat, then left Maddie and Logan on their own again. Maddie looked forward to Logan stealing another kiss, but the stream of people passing the van on their way to the restrooms and concession stand revealed the one problem of parking so close to the middle of the drive-in.

As stragglers hurried by while the outside lights dimmed to signal the start of the second feature, she ventured, "Where do the couples on dates park?"

Logan turned to her, and in the darkness she could see his teeth gleam. "You can usually find a line of vans on the back row."

"Ah."

"But when the lights go down on that second feature, anywhere is fine." He leaned toward her, and she bent over the cooler to meet him halfway. His lips, soft but insistent, probed hers, and she opened her mouth slightly to invite him in. They leaned forward more, pressing their bodies together, arms around each other as the kiss deepened and intensified. His hand cupped the nape of her neck, pulling her closer.

Behind Maddie, the side door slid open.

They both bolted upright and whirled around, to see a blurry eyed Faith crawl inside. "I'm getting cold," she explained. "Can I sit in here?"

Logan looked at Maddie. She already knew what the answer had to be and nodded, disappointed but amused. "Sure, kiddo," Logan told his daughter. "But you won't be able to see the movie as well."

"I'm not into superhero movies as much as Conner is." Faith wrapped a blanket around her and sat in the middle of the bench seat, behind Logan and Maddie. Then she did a double take. "Why are all the windows fogged up?"

"Must be humid out," Logan muttered, making Maddie giggle. His mouth quirked as he turned to her with a look of lust, which this time wasn't faked at all.


Somewhere uptown a clock rang midnight, while Maddie and Dena helped Logan unload his van. Faith managed to rouse herself enough to stumble into the house, but Logan cradled Conner, while Maddie hauled in the now-empty cooler. Dena carried a bag of trash, and a tub half full of uneaten popcorn.

99

In the front hallway they all milled around for a moment, in an uncertain group. Logan's mother had left the front porch light on, and a night light burned in the hallway, but the only sound was the ticking of a grandfather clock and the shuffling of feet.

"G'night." Faith gave each of the adults a hug and, still wrapped in a blanket, moved in slow motion up the stairs. The physical contact didn't bother Maddie nearly as much as it did a few days ago. Was that good? Or dangerous for all of them?

"She's so darling," Dena whispered. "But she has spirits around her, too."

Logan gave her a startled look. "What—"

"Good spirits," she assured him.

When Conner picked that moment to give out a little snore, Logan let it go. Instead, he gestured with his chin toward the bag Dena carried. "Just leave it by the door, I'll take care of it in the morning."

"Cool." Dena let the bag settle to the floor, then held the popcorn tub up with a hopeful expression.

"Yes, you may have the popcorn, young lady." Grinning, Logan turned to Maddie. "Usually I take classy dames like you to fancy restaurants."

Maddie looked away, not wanting to show her disappointment. Until this moment, she hadn't considered that this was a date, one that wouldn't end as she'd like. "I enjoyed our ... talk."

"If you'd like to stay awhile—"

Maddie shook her head, and felt a heaviness fall over her. Staying would lead to nothing good—and everything good. "You have your children to tuck in, and I have mine."

"Hey!" Dena hissed.

Logan reached out to muss Dena's hair. "Make sure you brush your teeth and wash behind your ears." Then he turned to Maddie and, holding Conner with both arms to keep the sleeping boy from keeling over, gave her a brief, warm kiss. "Next time."

Dena opened the door, but glanced back to say, "I'll baby-sit next time." Logan gave her a look of thanks.

As she followed Dena to her metallic green Porsche, Maddie wondered how there might be a next time, with what had to be done. She got behind the wheel and drove through quiet streets, feeling the stillness all the way through her body.

"It could still work," Dena said quietly.

"What could?"

"You know what. We've got time for damage control, and you haven't lied to him straight out, not yet."

Maddie shook her head. "It's too late for that—"

"Come on—you're a fighter. Break it to him slowly, grovel a lot, apologize two or three hundred times."

"That's your fight strategy?"

"It would be if I was the one guilty of sins of omission." When Maddie didn't speak, Dena continued. "Your ally is time. Make him fall in love with you, at the same time give him hints about why you're here, and eventually he'll forgive you. It's like this popcorn—butter it up and it'll taste better."

"That's the most ridiculous metaphor in the history of romance." But Maddie thought about it, and by the time she pulled into the hotel lot began to wonder if it might be possible. If she spent the week close to him—if he felt the same way she did—the most unlikely of possibilities could happen.

Maddie had a feeling Logan intended "next time" to be the next day, but he showed up at noon with the kids in tow—they'd overhead him saying Maddie's name, and went into full-blown pester mode until he took them along. Maddie's own "kid" was there, anyway, debating lunch plans with her when the Chandler clan walked through the door with pizza.

Maddie hadn't eaten pizza since college. She couldn't remember ever sitting on a bed to eat, surrounded by happy chatter instead of the clink of wine glasses and catty comments. It came as a surprise—a revelation—how much more fun it was. No networking, no social competition, no worries about image.

She didn't miss the hungry looks Logan kept giving her, as he sat on one end of the bed with everyone else between them. He clearly wanted it to be a bit less crowded.

That, Maddie told herself, was exactly why it shouldn't be. It was also why she jumped to say yes to another invitation to a Chandler family supper that evening. With Dena and the entire clan there, what she wanted to happen … wouldn't.

Still, she couldn't remember the last time she'd been so relaxed all day, except for those few times the guilt started to get to her.

Then she overslept the next morning, and woke to an empty room.

Rubbing the sleep from her face, Maddie hurried to the window. No Porsche. "Oh, Dena …" As she looked at the empty space, a van pulled in to fill it. A black van.

"Oh, dear." Maddie rushed to the door, unlocked it, then grabbed her suitcase and dashed into the bathroom. She was half dressed by the time the knock came. "It's open, come in!"

She peeked out to see Logan enter the room, alone. "I'm dressing."

"So, the opposite of what I'd hoped for." He wore a navy sports coat and slacks, a light blue button up shirt, and a tie.

"You own two ties!" She left the bathroom door cracked as she finished dressing, then started on her hair.

"One for meetings, one for Sunday."

Sunday ... tomorrow she had to go back to work. Maddie paused in the act of scrubbing her face with a washcloth. What was she doing?

"You okay in there?"

"Fine." She'd put on a white blouse and her shortest skirt—which wasn't too short, but still—and hurried to pull on pantyhose. "I'm putting on my face." She reached for her makeup bag.

"Don't take too long. The restaurant's just down the street, but the reservation is for eleven-thirty."

*The what?* She opened the door, to see him give her a longing once-over. "What reservation?"

Logan frowned. "You didn't send a note requesting a more formal date?"

"No ..." But Maddie knew who did.

"We've been conned, you and I. By my mother and your assistant, I'd wager." But instead of being angry, he broke into a grin. "This doesn't change the fact that I do have a reservation."

Maddie had reservations, too. She stepped out of the bathroom, trying to find a way to voice them, but could only say, "How expensive is this restaurant?"

He tilted his head, looking thoughtful. "The kids may have to go without food Monday, but it's doable. Kidding, don't worry about that—I'm what they call a successful small businessman. I don't even have to work weekends anymore." Logan walked toward her. "Worry about this."

He put his arms around Maddie, drew her into a kiss. She tried to protest, but only for a second before she forgot what she was going to protest about. Then she parted her lips and melted into him.

Logan's hands warmed her back, then wandered to her shoulders. He pushed her back for a second, started to say something about the reservations, then pulled her to him again. They fit perfectly. Maddie wondered why she'd never felt this way kissing a man before, not even her fiancé, what's-his-name. Maybe lawyers really did have no warmth.

It was Maddie's turn to push Logan away. "Reservations."

"What?" Looking confused, he stepped toward her again, but she firmly—and reluctantly—pushed him back.

"We eat first." He looked unconvinced. "Third date rule?"

He raised an eyebrow. "Huh? Oh. Well, we went to the drive-in twice, and dinner at my place …"

"Forget it, buster. The note very clearly said I wanted a more formal date. Even if I didn't write it."

Looking on the verge of a protest, he instead took her hand and led her toward the door. "Let's go before …" He left that hanging.

It turned out the restaurant was just down the street, and they walked there while Maddie felt every nerve sing at the idea of what "before" meant.

Everyone knew Logan, of course. They ended up in a corner booth of a restaurant Maddie wouldn't have looked twice at in Boston, a place catering at the moment to the after-church crowd. Its rustic decorations and home sports team photos spoke of warmth, and home.

Not that she noticed them much.

"I realize this is a bit beneath you." Logan waved a menu to indicate the place, then faltered.

*You were hoping I'd take the position beneath you, weren't you?* "There's something I don't believe you fully understand about me."

He leaned forward, looking both intrigued and worried. "You're not vegan …"

"Not since I first tasted the roast chicken at Hamersley's Bistro." She smiled at his surprise. "Which brings me to my point. There are trappings of my position that I enjoy, like—"

"The car?"

"Yes, my Porsche. Also, having a personal assistant, and I can't complain about the pay. And …" Her eyes went out of focus as she thought about it. What else did she like about her life? "The accoutrements that come with being a big city lawyer are part of the job. Well, to me they are—most of the partners would disagree."

"So … you don't like the fancy clothes and gourmet food?" Logan looked up as the waitress approached.

"The clothes are nice, but …" To demonstrate her point, Maddie tapped her menu. "Cheeseburger with everything and fries, please, and iced tea."

"I'll have the same." When the waitress left, Logan leaned back. "When did you last have a cheeseburger?"

"Don't be presumptuous. Dena brings them home, from time to time. At any rate, I'm used to the formal dinners and boardroom meetings, but that doesn't mean I like them. It's just what you do when you work for a law firm that serves wealthy clients."

Logan waited, a smile playing on his lips.

"Fine. I was in college when I last had a cheeseburger. Satisfied?"

"Torpedoing your diet just to be contrary." He reached out to take her hand. "So, why did you become a lawyer?"

He had a way of cutting straight to the chase. "I have to admit, it was partially to be successful, to be in control of my own life instead of depending on strangers. Being orphaned will do that to you."

"Other than sneaking burgers with Dena, is there anything in your life that isn't part of the job?"

She drew in a breath. "My life is … satisfying."

Logan squeezed her hand. "I could satisfy you better, and without three forks and a finger bowl."

"Of that I have no doubt." Her imagination supplied the rest. Still, a feeling of foreboding edged in throughout the meal, despite food ten times better than anything she'd tried at a dinner party. The company was ten times better, too.

She tried to ignore the feeling, despite knowing exactly where it came from. Her emotions battled her better judgment, and the fact that she sat here with Logan Chandler meant the better judgment was losing.

They were quiet, talked out, by the time they headed back toward the hotel. Or maybe not so much talked out as anticipating. Maddie again pushed her misgivings away and thought of the empty room awaiting them.

Dena stood by the hotel's front door, gripping a briefcase and looking scared. As Maddie approached, the other woman grabbed her by the arm and took her aside. "Plan Commission meeting. It hit the front page of today's newspaper, and guess who's listed as representing the development company?" She produced a newspaper from behind the briefcase, holding it so Logan couldn't see. The headline was above the fold.

*So. This is it.* Maddie turned to Logan, who stood by with a look of concern. "Are you okay? You look ill."

It had to end. What happened to her commitment to truth?

*Like pulling off a bandage.* "I tried to tell you the first day … my law firm is doing the legal work for the development company." At his confused look she added, "The company that wants to buy the drive-in. It's mostly paperwork, but I have to give the rezoning presentation to the county Plan Commission." Then, because even to her own ears it sounded like the worst betrayal imaginable, she added, "I'm sorry."

Logan stared at her, his mouth open. When her words finally registered, his jaw snapped shut, fists clenched, and a red hue flooded his face.

What else could she have expected?

Dena stepped between her boss and their new worst nightmare and took a fighting stance, the briefcase held out in front of her. "You touch her and you'll regret it."

Logan folded his arms and regarded the much smaller woman. "What are you going to do, invade my home town and suck all the happiness out? Oh, wait—you already did that. Maybe now you'd like to ban Harry Potter and cancel Christmas."

"Dena, down." Maddie grabbed her friend by the arm and dragged her out of the way, so she could face Logan. "I want you to know I respect your beliefs—"

That didn't have the desired effect. Logan's face turned even more red and he flung his arms out. "Another lie?"

"I never lied to you!"

"Every minute since we met has been a lie. You've been spying on me since the moment you maneuvered your way into my van, that first night at the drive-in."

"Spying?" Maddie's legs almost gave out. It was much worse than she'd thought, and worst of all, her law firm condoned—or at least, ignored—exactly that kind of behavior. How could she convince him she didn't do what she might well have done before they met?

Logan stabbed a shaking finger at her. "I expected underhanded tactics when I heard an outside law firm had been called in. But you used my children—my *children*—to get into my life and undermine the opposition. That's not business, it's personal."

"Logan, I would never do that. I would never—"

"Then why didn't you tell me why you were here?"

"I—" *Why indeed?* "I didn't know you lead the opposition, when we first met. By the time I found out—" She faltered, having no good reason for not coming clean immediately.

"You just happened to climb into the van of the guy who organized the opposition to your plan?"

"It isn't *my* plan—"

"You just happened to get involved in my life? To take my

attention away from the development? You just happened to have a van that looked exactly like mine?"

"Yes!" Maddie cried. "That's what coincidence is."

"I should know better than to expect a straight answer from a lawyer." He turned, but after two steps whirled back on her. "As God is my witness, you'll never touch that property, and you'll never come close to me and mine. You stay away from my family! If you hurt my kids, so help me ..." He stalked toward his van.

Maddie didn't watch him go. She turned and, with carefully controlled strides, walked into the hotel, while Dena trailed behind her. Only when they reached their room did she allow herself to collapse, falling onto a chair.

Dena put an arm around her shoulders. "We'll show that—that—man what a real fight is like. He can't say those things about you without paying for it, right?"

"Right." But Maddie's heart wasn't in it. She wondered how it could ever be in anything again.

# CHAPTER SEVEN

"But why can't we see Maddie anymore?"

Logan's hand jerked, and a spoonful of freshly ground coffee flew across the mixing table to land in a jar of blend he'd just finished. He turned toward his daughter, who was helping Lydia frost freshly baked rolls across the coffee shop's back room. Lydia, looking more like a disapproving aunt than his only employee, raised an eyebrow while Logan counted slowly to ten.

"You just mixed that, Dad," said Conner, who stood by the mixing table and almost took the grounds full in the face. "Will that ruin the blend?"

"Probably," Logan told him, as he grasped the edge of the wooden table and squeezed.

Conner picked up a stirring rod and, concentrating hard, began to mix the black grounds into the brownish-red mix. "Maybe I can fix it. Why can't we see Maddie anymore?"

Logan started counting again.

Lydia, a sheen of sweat making her dark skin shine, turned to give Logan an appraising look, with something approaching a smirk. "Conner, the rolls are ready. Can you help your sister take them out to the display case?"

"'Kay. But don't throw away my new blend."

"We wouldn't dream of it, baby." Lydia waited until Conner and Faith disappeared through the swinging door, then whipped out a towel and began to clean frosting from her table. That kept her back to Logan on the other side of the large kitchen, but he could still hear her chuckle.

"What? Don't you want to ask me why we can't see Maddie anymore?" He picked up the ruined mix and started to toss it into the trash despite Conner's request, just to show who was in charge. Then, after a moment's hesitation, he poured it into an empty coffee maker and started brewing.

"Oh, I understand why you don't want to see Maddie." Lydia turned to face him, and Logan couldn't stand the sympathy he saw. "Everyone was already in love with her, and she turns out to be the enemy. Why try to salvage that, when it'll likely break your heart even more? Maybe I'd take the safe route too."

"Yeah." Well, at least somebody understood where he was coming from.

"On the other hand, I saw the look in your eyes when you talked about her."

"That tune again, huh? Please, once more—with feeling." Logan turned away from her to stare at the stream of hot coffee filling the pot beside him, as if it held the secret of life. Why couldn't anyone understand they'd been betrayed? It wasn't just that he'd lost Maddie— he'd never had her. She'd played the worst kind of cruel trick, taking his heart, only to hand it back damaged.

He was still staring a moment later, when his mother walked in and looked over his shoulder. "That smells rich. Is it a new blend?"

"I'll tell you in a minute."

"Well, I hope you've given up on the Cherry Bean Blend. It tasted like a cough drop. Honestly, do these ideas come in dreams after a big dinner?"

When he didn't answer, Judy caught the undercurrent. "Lydia, were you—?"

"Yep."

"Oh, Liddy, leave the poor boy alone while the wound is so fresh. He'll realize soon enough that Maddie is as much a victim as he is."

"What?"

Judy crossed her arms, fixing Logan with the same glare she'd used when he came home wearing muddy clothes. "Do you really think she invaded your personal life as part of some huge conspiracy?"

Although tired of arguing the point, Logan had to admit his reputation for pursuing his position to the bitter end was well earned. "The airport is a multimillion dollar investment, and the people making that investment will do whatever it takes to get the cash flowing."

"I haven't seen such paranoia since the Cold War." Judy smiled. "Not that I remember that far back."

"Do you honestly think all that—climbing into the wrong van, just by chance walking into my shop—was a coincidence?"

"Dear, that's what coincidence is."

"The next person who tells me that, I swear—" Logan stopped short when he realized the last person had been Maddie. "Mom, she's a lawyer."

"The way you say that, it sounds like we should lock her in a secret lab with an electric probe inserted in her brain."

"If the shoe fits—"

They were interrupted by Lydia, which didn't surprise Logan. She'd watched him as a kid and now, as an employee, still didn't hesitate to cut him down to size. "You know, there was a time when my people were stereotyped as a group."

She stared at him, and he returned her gaze with the knowledge that he couldn't meet that argument. "Fine. But surely you can't compare lawyers to ... bakery chefs."

Lydia gave a startled laugh, waved him off, and returned to her work. "That coffee smells good," she said over her shoulder.

Turning to the pot, Logan saw it was full of a reddish tinged fluid that did, indeed, have a wonderful aroma. But he'd been fooled before, and suspected the taste would be less than perfect, at best.

That made him think of Maddie again.

Judy apparently hadn't stopped thinking of Maddie, because the older woman still stood a few feet away, giving him a cold stare. "Maddie is a good person."

"Mom—"

"I'm an excellent judge of character—"

"And so modest."

"—and I know she's a good person at heart. Besides, if she wasn't a good person, why would my grandchildren—and their father—be so attracted to her?"

"Character flaws?" Wanting desperately to drop the subject, Logan grabbed the pot and poured a half cup of coffee, then held it out to his mother. "Here, it's decaf. Most of it."

Judy ignored it. "You're the coffee tester around here. Meanwhile, the children are still asking why their new friend can't talk to them anymore, and you need to address that."

"What am I supposed to say? That I'm afraid she'll shove another knife into my gut and twist it?"

"Why not tell the truth? They can't see Maddie again because you're unable to separate your love life from your public life."

To keep from screaming in frustration, Logan took a swallow of the ruined coffee mix. It took him a moment to realize the mixture not only tasted good, but slid down his throat like nectar straight from heaven.

Shaking his head, he turned to pour each woman a cup. "Ladies, I'd like to introduce you to the Conner Mix." Maybe that would turn their minds away from his personal life for a while.

Judy and Lydia exchanged looks, then each took a cup. They continued glancing at each other, like school children on a dare, then sipped at the same time. Two pairs of eyes opened wide, and two pairs of lips curved into contented smiles.

But Judy refused to let it go. Taking another swallow, she said, "Just imagine—you assumed, despite how nice it seemed to the senses, that this would be no good, but it turned out fine."

"Oh, for—"

The door burst open and Conner came in, carrying an empty tray. He tossed it into the sink and demanded, "Dad, why can't we see Maddie anymore?"

With a sigh, Logan held out his cup. "Son, your new coffee is a hit."

As Logan hoped, Conner forgot everything else and sniffed the new mix, then peppered the women with questions about its taste, and where it should go on the menu. But just when Logan started to breathe more easily Faith came in, handed Judy a stack of mail, and turned an injured look on her father.

"Why?"

Okay, that was it. Logan reached out and grabbed the cup from Conner, then took Faith's arm to line the two children up. He addressed them and their grandmother, who sorted through the mail but also kept an eye on her family.

"Now, look: I've already told you, Maddie works for the company that wants to tear down the drive-in. It's not that I have anything against Maddie, but she's fighting for one thing and we're fighting for something else—you want to save the drive-in, right?" The kids nodded solemnly. "We all do. And I can't risk being distracted by making friends with someone who's trying to wreck it. So, until this is over, I will have absolutely no contact with Maddie at all, except when I have to at meetings and such. Understand?"

Again Faith and Conner nodded, although they both looked less than certain and a bit rebellious. Still, Logan decided he could settle for that if they would just stop berating him for one lousy hour. "Well, then ... we'll talk about it again once the fight is over."

In a very small voice Conner asked, "Are you and Maddie going to hit each other?"

Lydia gave a barely audible giggle.

Kneeling down, Logan gathered his children in his arms. "No, not that kind of fight. It will be lots of talk and paperwork, and no one will hit anyone."

"Will it be over by next weekend?" Faith asked. "There's a triple feature."

"No, babe, I'm afraid it won't be that quick." If only it could be. If only Logan could look forward to some kind of closure, both with the

116

drive-in and with Maddie, without the drawn out torture of a legal battle. But at least he could avoid Maddie, and try to get her out of his mind.

If only he could get her out of his heart.

"Oh, my," Judy said.

Logan looked up to see her examine the contents of a manila envelope she'd just opened. This can't be good, he thought, although Judy's expression could have reflected horror or amusement. "What is it?"

"Well ..." She looked at him over a stack of papers. "Remember when you asked me to find a renter for the empty office space upstairs, to help with the legal fees? The good news is, the company I've been corresponding with has finished the rental contract, and everything's set."

"That's good." Logan climbed to his feet and waited. Rarely did someone say "the good news is" without adding some bad news. "So, what's the company?"

"It turns out they're a law firm—from Boston."

Logan tensed. "Boston?"

"Not *that* law firm," his mother added quickly. "But ... it's Quincy, Dixon and Tremayne."

"Oh." Why did that name sound familiar? Quincy, Dixon and Tremayne? Where—? "*Oh.*"

"They'll be moving in directly." Judy glanced at the kids, who appeared to know something was wrong, but not what. "Directly upstairs."

Logan didn't know whether to laugh or cry. He did know, without a doubt, that the rental contract would be ironclad and unbreakable. It could hardly be otherwise. As he sank into a chair, every muscle turned to rubber, he heard Maddie's words ring like an alarm in his head:

"That's what coincidence is."

"Well," Dena breathed, "isn't this a big karmic laugh riot."

Maddie could only manage: "We're moving where?"

Tupper stood in the hotel suite and looked from her to Dena, apparently unaware of why his boss turned so suddenly upset. "Um, it's a good location downtown. The office area's real nice—I helped move some old books out of there when I was a kid."

He hesitated, and Maddie realized she must be wearing a deer in the headlights look. She slid into an office chair and made an effort to compose herself, then asked Tupper to repeat the address. He looked to the contract and spoke slowly, as if unsure what he could be doing wrong.

Of course Maddie knew the address, from the front door of a certain coffee shop downtown. Of course.

"Wow," Dena murmured, from her position behind her desk. "Fate is putting in some overtime."

Tupper shifted uncomfortably. "I know it's on the second floor, but maybe the company could have an elevator installed or something ... they make great coffee downstairs."

"So I've heard," Maddie said dryly. "And can I assume this is the company's usual unbreakable contract?"

Tupper leafed through the contract, his lips moving as he studied the fine print. "Um, ninety day notice on either side, so we'd have to pay them for three months if we moved out—but why would we? It's a good spot."

"Did you read the newspaper article about the Plan Commission meeting?"

"Newspapers give me a headache. I'm reading the new Oz book right now, it's really good. Did you know they still put those out? I wonder if it's the same writer."

Maddie shook her head. "If I want fantasy, I'll imagine a happy ending in real life." Amazing. Tupper seemed to be the only person around who didn't know what was going on, and when he figured it out she'd lose one more ally. In the days since that newspaper article they'd received critical and even threatening calls and e-mails, and the hotel had to be evacuated after a bomb threat that police traced to her presence. In fact...

Maddie gave Dena a speculative look. "There might be an advantage to moving in there, besides the location."

But Dena was way ahead of her. "No more terrorism?"

"We can only hope." And no more cowardly running from her problems. Standing, Maddie swept a quick look around the room and snapped her fingers. "Tupper, get us a moving truck."

"You might not understand the irony, dear, but this used to be a law office." Judy waved her hand to take in the reception area, brightly lit by the sun beaming in through three wide windows.

Maddie nodded; the place screamed Attorney. It looked bare, with the floor stripped of carpeting and no curtains or furniture, but she liked the hardwood floor and the high ceiling. She followed Judy on a tour through two individual offices, a library with empty but dust free shelves, a kitchen, and a large bathroom, and decided she liked it just fine.

The smell of fresh coffee and rolls, wafting through vents from downstairs, helped—but also hurt.

They paused again in the reception area. "I don't understand why this place hasn't been in use before, Judy," Dena said, as she efficiently examined the area in advance of the movers. "It's got real character."

Judy hesitated. "When Marty—that is, Martin Dunn, who owns the drive-in—invited us to move to Indiana, he helped my husband find this place to start the shop again."

Again? Maddie wondered what happened before, but Judy seemed so hesitant to tell the story at all that she dropped the issue.

"We bought it from an attorney who retired, and Ralph, my husband, used the upstairs for storage and office space for a short time. But he said it smelled like lawyer—I'm sorry, Maddie—and it's been empty ever since. Ralph always said withholding this space from some attorney was his small bit of revenge."

Maddie glanced at Dena, who had stopped to hear the story. Her friend opened her mouth to ask questions, saw Maddie's warning look, and reluctantly went back to work. Maddie knew how she felt—clearly, she'd only heard half a story, but her instincts told her Judy didn't want to tell the rest.

Judy's eyes glazed over for a moment, then refocused. "Ralph will probably spin in his grave, God rest his soul, but maybe he would take some comfort in knowing the money you'll pay us will go toward fighting you. Isn't that something?"

"Ironic," Maddie agreed. "Judy … I can't tell you how sorry I am—"

The older woman patted her on the arm. "I know it's not personal. And I know how you feel about Logan."

"How can you, when I don't?" Sometimes she thought she did ... and that's when she really got scared.

"Things will work out, dear."

"But if I win, Logan will never forgive me, and if I lose, my career is over." Maddie heard the desperation in her own voice, and mentally kicked herself for showing weakness.

It didn't faze Judy a bit. "When the Good Lord closes a door—" She paused, then touched Maddie's arm. "Well, sometimes it means you weren't meant to walk through it. I have to go, but I'll send some lunch up for you later." She made her exit just as two overall clad movers lurched up the inside staircase, hauling the first piece of furniture.

The morning passed quickly after that, as the workers unloaded a small truck while Maddie, Dena, and Tupper organized and hooked up their equipment. In Maddie's opinion it looked pathetic when they finished: one small desk in the reception area, overwhelmed by the size of the room, and another in her office, which left the second office, kitchen, and library bare of furniture. The only thing left was the folding table to hold the copier and other electronic equipment, which went to one corner of the reception area, and the file cabinet Dena placed by her desk.

"It still looks empty," Tupper complained after the movers left. "There's no furniture in my office at all. Isn't there supposed to be something to channel the chi, or chai, or something?"

Dena, who'd crawled behind her desk to hook up her computer, climbed out and gave him a big hug. "Tupper, your aura is simply irresistible."

"Thanks, I made it myself."

Maddie had to smile, which might have been her first all week. But her smile faded moments later when the front door opened, and two familiar faces appeared.

Faith and Conner marched in, but they weren't alone. Behind them, quickly filling the reception area despite its size, trooped an army of children—two dozen at least, the oldest in their early teens and the youngest half that. All wore somber expressions, and Faith held a manila envelope.

Maddie took a breath. Glad as she was to see Faith and Conner, she hadn't been a room with this many kids since she was one, herself.

Ignoring Maddie, Faith walked up to Dena and said, "Could I speak to the person in charge, please?"

"Of course." Dena took her seat, picked up the phone, and punched the intercom button—even though they hadn't hooked up an intercom. "Miss McKinley, you have visitors in the reception area." She pretended to listen, then spoke to Faith. "Ms. McKinley will be with you in a moment."

"Thank you." Without a glance at Maddie, Faith turned to Tupper. "Good afternoon." The other children looked on in silence.

"Good afternoon," Tupper replied, sounding serious despite the grin splitting his face. "That's a handsome outfit you're wearing today, Miss Chandler. Is it new?"

Faith glanced down at her dress, a burgundy affair with lace sleeves. "It's from Easter."

All right, then. Clearly, this was not a social visit, and the rules had been established. Maddie turned on her heels, walked through the inner hallway to her office, then spun around and reentered the reception area. "Hello, ladies and gentlemen. What can I do for you?"

Stepping forward, Faith handed her the envelope and took a deep breath. "We're here on behalf of all the families of Hopewell, Noble County, and the surrounding area, to present this petition."

Maddie opened the envelope and pulled out a stack of lined paper, filled with signatures ranging from careful printing to chicken scratches.

"We the undersigned," Faith said, having obviously memorized the words of the petition, "ask that you cease in your efforts to replace our beloved drive-in with an airport. This is our favorite place to be and holds many good memories, and we believe it would cause great harm to our community to lose it."

Conner stepped up beside his sister and added, "It would be like losing Christmas." Clearly, someone had coached Conner on that line, which Maddie told herself was far too sentimental to be taken seriously. That didn't stop Dena from drawing a ragged breath.

Maddie looked down at the names and tried to read them, but the signatures blurred no matter how much she tried to blink her vision clear. She didn't celebrate Christmas, hadn't for a long time. She lost Christmas when her sister died.

"Kids, I—" She cleared her throat, tried to start again, and faltered. As she tried to regain control—where did it go, so suddenly?—another voice drowned out the roaring in her ears.

"*You're* trying to shut down the drive-in?" Tupper's voice rose to a squeak. "You mean—*this* company is building the airport?" He stared at Maddie as if he'd found an insect in his lunch. "I've been helping you!"

"You didn't know, Tupper," Dena told him, but he refused to be soothed.

"You can have my office back! And—and this!" He yanked a paycheck from his pocket and slammed it down on the table. "No, wait, I need that." Grabbing it back, he stuffed it into the pocket of his plaid shirt and shook his fist. "Because I'll use it to help fight you! We'll all fight you! You tell my uncle—both my uncles—to shove it up their—"

When he realized the kids hung on his every word, Tupper faltered. "Their noses! Yeah. I'll help the kids, and we'll tell the adults what's going on, too. We'll tell Logan right now, then he'll know what you're really like. Come on, group!"

Confused by the sudden turn of events, and mostly because he was the first adult to throw his hat into their ring, the children turned to file out after a still ranting Tupper. Conner turned to wave, and Faith gave Maddie an apologetic look as she headed up the rear.

Maddie listened to the clamber of stomping feet and grumbling voices headed down the stairs. In the emptiness that followed, she found her way to a folding chair and sank down beside Dena's desk.

"So." Dena cleared her throat. "This is how it feels to be the underdog."

This was, Maddie decided, the second worse week of her life. She looked at Dena, but dared not speak while she struggled for self-control, and reminded herself that losing it got her into this position to begin with.

"On the brighter side," Dena told her after still another silence, "Tupper's up to speed on the whole thing about you being an underhanded, slimy lawyer."

"We should always seek to keep our employees educated." Maddie folded her arms on the desk, dropped her head onto them, and murmured, "'In my many years I have come to a conclusion that one useless man is a shame, two is a law firm, and three or more is a congress.'"

"John Adams? And we're the shameful law firm?" Dena ventured. Maddie nodded. "Well, at least we're not a congress."

Maddie nodded again. "All this leads us to the obvious question of what else could possibly go wrong."

Her cell phone rang.

"Oh, Maddie. How could you ask that?"

"Madison McKinley."

"What's your status?" Adam Quincy sounded angry for having to ask. "Are you moved in to your new office?"

"We just finished, Mr. Quincy." Maddie saw Dena roll her eyes. "Ironically, it's right above a shop owned by the leader of the opposition."

"Oh?" Quincy chuckled, which from him sounded like the chortle of a movie villain. "Well, keep your ear to the floor."

Maybe he was in a good mood, if that was possible. As long as they were talking ears, she decided to put a bug in his. "I'm having my doubts about our actions in this matter."

"Don't have doubts," he barked. "Have success."

So much for a good mood. "I understand the financial risks, but this could turn into a public relations disaster. The drive-in has overwhelming support. We face an upcoming Plan Commission meeting, and then a City Council vote that will likely go against us, if the elected officials want to stay in the good graces of their constituents."

"Hm. The democratic process can be a damn nuisance in cases like this." Quincy paused, considering. "Have you spoken to the drive-in's owner yet?"

"I've seen him." Pictures of him. True enough, if not a literal answer to the question.

"Well, turn on your womanly charm, then offer him lots of money, a retirement home in Hawaii, a woman of loose morals, whatever. If we can get him to sign on the dotted line, the problem's over."

"I doubt that will solve the entire problem—"

"Sure it will. He sells, we raze the drive-in, and there's nothing to argue over anymore. Then the vote will go our way because nobody will oppose it."

"But the community will lose a part of their heritage."

"I'm in Boston, do I care about their heritage?" Quincy paused, then his voice hardened. "McKinley, remember which side your bread is buttered on. Are you going soft on me?"

"No sir, I am not." Maddie wondered how much of a lie that was.

"This is about taking care of our clients, not about whether somebody will have to buy a Blu-ray player. Stay the course and do what I pay you to do, if you value your career."

"Mr. Quincy, I'm not—" But the line went dead.

Maddie jammed the phone into her purse and turned to meet Dena's expectant gaze. "It seems the partners care about nothing but earning their fee."

"This surprises you why?"

She shook her head, unable to deny Dena's meaning. "Compromise isn't on the table. Quincy sees no possibility that doesn't involve a lost case or a landing strip, and I'm not sure he's wrong. How can there be a compromise? Use the drive-in to light the runway?"

"Maybe they could project the in-flight movie into the planes," Dena suggested with a gentle smile.

But Maddie didn't see any humor in it. "I've seen the plans. The airplanes will touch down in row ten—twenty feet from the concession stand."

"That," said a voice from the doorway, "Is bound to disturb the customers."

They looked up to see Logan, a paper bag in one hand, a cup carrier in the other, and a murderous look in his eyes.

# CHAPTER EIGHT

Logan stalked into the room like a soldier on patrol, eyeing every corner as if searching for booby traps. "Haven't been up here for a while." He was dressed down, for him, in jeans, black running shoes, and a red T-shirt with the words "More Coffee!" emblazoned in white on the front. "Hasn't changed much."

Maddie started to feel faint, realized she was holding her breath, and deliberately controlled her respiration before speaking. "I saw no point in making it ... homey." She gestured toward Dena. "If you're here about the rental agreement, my assistant deals with questions of paperwork. But I assure you—"

"It's an ironclad contract, I know." He shook the paper bag. "Lunch. My mother suffered a convenient headache and couldn't make the delivery."

"How coincidental," Dena murmured. She'd been staring at Logan with enough fascination to give Maddie a flash of jealousy, but now she stood up. "I have to be in the kitchen."

Turning so quickly she almost threw herself out of her chair, Maddie grabbed her friend's arm. "What for?"

"Measuring."

"Measuring?"

Dena nodded. "We need furniture—tables, chairs, a microwave—I mean, the menu from downstairs is extremely limited, and suppose they decide to poison the food? I need to make sure what'll fit before I place an order."

"Take one with you." Logan held the drink carrier, which held two cups, out toward her.

Maddie caught Dena's eye and shook her head.

"I'll try it." Shaking Maddie off, Dena took the cup, cast another sidelong look at Logan, then beat a hasty retreat.

Maddie heard "Bleh!" from the hallway, then "I didn't think he'd really poison us!" before a door closed.

Logan looked after Dena, his expression distressed. "Everyone liked my lemon coffee, so I thought I was on a roll."

*Peachy*, Maddie thought. Logan still stood in the middle of the room, holding the bag and looking everywhere except at her. Ah, well—it seemed the week for uncomfortable confrontations, why stop now? "Did Tupper find you?"

"Yeah. He's come over from the dark side." Logan cleared his throat. "I didn't know the kids were coming up here, by the way."

"I'm quite sure you told them to stay away from me." When he didn't deny it, she took a deep breath, trying to throw off the heavy feeling that came over her. Wasn't that what she'd wanted? To avoid children?

"Yeah, I—they went off to make signs. I think they're planning to picket." He shrugged. "I tried to tell them picketing this building meant they'd be picketing me, too ..."

Maddie stood long enough to take the bag—although she left him holding the coffee. She swept paperwork from the desk into an empty drawer to leave room for plastic containers of sandwiches, vegetables, and fruit. "I suppose I'll have to eat at my desk."

"Beats the floor." He looked around yet again, then cleared his throat. "There's enough there for both of you."

"I appreciate that, but Dena always prepares her own food—heavy on the sprouts and leafy vegetables."

"New age stuff."

"So—would you like some?" Their gazes locked, and Maddie wondered who was more amazed at the offer. "I see no reason why we can't be ... amicable." *Oh, this is a bad, bad idea.*

"You don't, huh?" With a half-smile, Logan took Dena's vacated chair. He carefully laid the drink carrier out of Maddie's reach, then reached for a sandwich. "I do see some advantage in keeping an eye on you."

"Keep your enemies close, yes."

"Yes." He brought the sandwich halfway to his mouth, then laid it down again and picked up the coffee cup. "Once more into the breach ..." He took a sip, swallowed, and set the cup down. "Okay, scratch root beer coffee."

"You're kidding."

He shook his head. "I wanted to apologize."

"For soft drink flavored coffee?"

"No—"

"For your accusations?"

"For losing my temper."

"I see." So the accusations stood, then. Maddie felt her own temper start to rise.

"You see, I've spent my entire adult life trying to stay even-tempered. I even took anger management classes."

That didn't give him an excuse; Maddie took a deep breath, and tried to force her own anger down. "Really? We have something else in common: The firm 'suggested' I take anger management classes, too. Who did you throw a glass at?"

Logan looked away. "Back in high school, I attacked a guy."

"You—what?" She stared at him, meal forgotten.

"It was the football playoffs, and I saw him put our quarterback—my best friend, my pastor now—out of action with a late hit from behind."

"Out of action?"

Logan shook himself. "I went crazy, attacked the guy while Jake was still lying there on the field. It took the whole team to pull me off. Then he showed up by the ambulance and tried to apologize. I broke his nose. I got cuffed and almost arrested—did get suspended, and wasn't there for my friend that night. Jake's been in a wheelchair ever since." Finally Logan met her gaze, and she saw the shame and sorrow burning in his eyes. "I tell that story about as often as you tell yours. You understand."

Yes, Maddie thought, she did. No wonder Logan had been so understanding when she told him about her sister. "Logan, I—"

"Just ... let's just eat. Don't let it get cold."

She decided not to point out that nothing in the meal had been hot.

As she ate Maddie kept remembering the wheelchair bound pastor she'd seen in the coffee shop, someone she'd not thought twice about. The silence became more oppressive until she burst out, "When our country was first founded, the Presidential candidate who got the second largest number of votes became the Vice-President."

For a long moment, he stared at her. "To coin a phrase: Huh?"

She'd thought the same thing, herself, but forged on. "After George Washington refused a third term, John Adams ran against Thomas Jefferson, and won. Because Jefferson got the second largest number of votes, he became Vice-President. They were political opposites, and came to hate each other, but they had to work together."

"Again with the 'huh'?"

"Well, they did work together, and in time even became close friends. I'd meant to draw parallels with our situation, but on second thought, shut up and eat." She bent her head down and attacked her food, hoping he didn't see how mortified she was for letting herself babble on.

But was it possible? Could they be ... close friends?

"That was either the clunkiest attempt to change the subject I've ever heard, or a brilliant commentary on—something."

She shoved the last bite of sandwich into her mouth and mumbled incoherently.

"Coincidence is what it's all about, isn't it?"

Startled, Maddie looked up from her meal. "What does that have to do with John Adams?"

"Nothing. I'm changing the subject myself, because you're obviously embarrassed at that un-lawyerlike speech. Anyway, Mom gets a *coincidental* migraine that forces me to come up here."

"Ah. Perhaps she took a chapter from my alleged crimes." She took a bite of fruit, mostly to keep from launching another disjointed speech, and waited to see how he would respond.

"That's what I mean. If our meeting really was chance, then the last week has been a series of amazing coincidences. If not ..."

If not, Maddie must be lying. He let that possibility hang, while he finished his own meal.

Maddie decided she needed to stick with the truth—which, she realized, fell under the heading of 'irony'. "It's difficult for me to defend myself, because I don't believe in fate."

"It's hard for me to be certain of your guilt, because I do."

"However, coincidence is a documented—" She paused when his last comment sank in. Before she could decide whether to be encouraged, he spoke again.

"Indulge me." Logan waved a carrot stick like a sword. "I've been getting abused pretty badly over the whole coincidence issue. It turns out Tupper was working both sides without even realizing it, which seems to me like the straw that broke the coincidental camel's back."

"Granted." Appetite gone, Maddie pushed the rest of her meal aside. "Why don't we stop circling the issue? I never met Tupper until that first day, the day I arrived here and met you, and I had no idea he worked at the drive-in. You can accuse me all you want of not telling the whole truth, but I didn't plan this, either."

"Okay." He continued looking at her and munched his sandwich, waiting for her to continue.

Even if he did decide to believe her, it didn't solve their personal dilemma. "We have to fight each other regardless, don't we?"

He shrugged. "We're stuck here together, fighting for different

134

sides, just like Adams and Jefferson. Unless you quit the fight."

*Quit?* "I can't do that." Maddie wondered what it would be like, to quit something because she didn't agree with it.

"Why not?" Logan's voice remained even, but his eyes flashed.

"Because it wouldn't be right."

Now his voice did rise. "Not right? Saying no to something that isn't right wouldn't be right? Do you detect the irony?"

"I would lose my job—everything I've worked toward—"

"Maybe you've worked toward the wrong thing."

"You don't know what I've done!" Maddie slammed her fist down, sending vegetables flying. "You don't know how hard I've worked, or what I've sacrificed. You're so sure of your own moral superiority, but you have no idea what my life was like before a week ago, or what I've been through. Have you ever heard of the glass ceiling? Have you ever heard—?"

"I hear a voice telling me to kiss you right now."

That shut her up. She stared at him, wondering if her ears deceived her, then realized his eyes had focused on her lips. She licked them, before thinking of how that might look.

"I had a few days to think about it, to calm down and trust my gut, and my family. I believe in fate—or coincidence. I believe you."

"I'm ... gratified."

"I can taste your lips," Logan continued, looking up to meet her eyes. "They're sweet and warm and moist, and I could spend the rest of my days kissing you."

"Oh." Maddie swallowed, unsure what else to say. What would that be like, to sink so totally into someone that nothing else mattered? To e-mail in her resignation and spend the rest of her life exploring the depths of a relationship, to make *them* more important than him or her?

Her inner voice screamed that it would make her a failure, someone who gave up and didn't finish what she started. Someone who would turn her back on responsibility.

Someone who wasn't there when her sister died.

With a gasp Maddie leaped out of her chair, and it fell over to clatter on the floor beside her. Logan also got up, his face reflecting concern, but when he reached out she drew back. "No. I can't—I have a commitment."

Exasperated, Logan waved his arms. "A commitment to what? Ruining innocent lives? Driving a family out of business after half a century?"

A third voice broke in, seemingly off the subject: "Your sister's death doesn't make you responsible for everything, Maddie."

They turned to see Dena at the entrance of the hallway, regarding them with a frown. "You've punished yourself long enough. Do something because it's right, not because it's some kind of self-defeating duty."

"You don't know what you're talking about."

"I know better than anyone," Dena insisted. "You saved me once, now I'm trying to save you."

"I don't need saving! I need to do my *job*." Maddie turned to Logan, desperate to keep this from ending the way she knew it must. "I have to. It's my commitment. Please understand."

But Logan shook his head. "No, that I don't understand. And until

136

one of us figures it out, we have nothing more to talk about." With that, he turned and marched toward the door.

It was Dena who stopped him, with a shout. Casting a sideways glance at Maddie, she joined Logan by the door and gestured for him to come closer, then whispered in his ear while Maddie wondered what was going on.

All the color rushed from Logan's face. He stumbled back, staring at Dena with wide eyes. Dena gave him an appealing look, then opened the door and waited until he took three steps into the outer hallway, his eyes on her the whole time. As the door closed Maddie saw Logan, mouth open in shock, still staring—not at her, but at her friend.

"What did you tell him?" Maddie demanded after they listened to his hesitant steps tap down the stairs.

Looking profoundly disturbed, Dena leaned against the door and hugged herself. "I told him to consult a higher authority."

Maddie waited for an explanation, but none came. This was ridiculous. As much as events already spiraled out of control, she couldn't have her assistant join the insanity just when she needed help the most. Disgusted—mostly with herself—Maddie grabbed her purse and headed for the door.

"Where are you off to?"

"To do my job. Your vibes, and Logan's idealism, won't get this deal made, so I will. Then we can get out of here and return to our real lives."

As the door closed behind her, Maddie heard Dena say, "Define 'real'," but she had no patience to turn back for a philosophical discussion. She, as usual, had work to do.

Logan shoved through the back door without a word to anyone, confident Lydia would keep an eye on the kids—and that his mother would experience a complete recovery and return to the shop in an hour or so. His body drove the van on automatic, north on Highway 3, while his mind barely functioned at all.

A few miles from town he turned onto a narrow country road, then past ornate cast iron gates, before he parked on an even narrower lane. His mind only came awake when he moved quietly through a hilly field that sprouted a variety of crosses and headstones, with the occasional concrete angel thrown in. It took a few minutes to reach the crest of a small rise, guarded by a trio of pines that kept silent watch over the Chandler family plot.

The plot covered a small area, since his family came to Indiana only a few decades before—and hadn't they all been so young at the time? His father's grave was a plain white cross, well taken care of by his family, and decorated every Memorial Day by the local VFW. Near the cross, at the top of the rise, sat a cement love seat which looked out over the rest of the cemetery.

Logan sank down onto it, and wondered again at how wise his mother had been to place it there. What more peaceful spot could there be in the world? A brick wall lined the area near the front gates, with a grove of trees alongside, so even though he could see part of the road in the distance traffic was barely a whisper. The Chandler plot lay near one side of the cemetery, so from his vantage he could see nothing else but trees and gravesites, broken by the edge of a wheat field in the distance.

Logan's attention rested a bit closer, on a tombstone directly before him. He couldn't see the carved writing, but it was impossible to forget: "Lisette Chandler, loving wife and mother". Simple, direct, just as she liked it.

And the dates, of course. She'd be thirty-six now, but to him Lise was frozen in time.

"Hello, Lise."

He waited, just in case. Then, feeling foolish, he cleared his throat. "I've come here more often than usual, lately. I suppose you'd hate that, but I've been troubled, and I needed to talk. It's not that I don't have friends ..." he smiled despite himself, remembering Lise once told him that if he got too wrapped up in his immediate family he'd lose all his friends.

When had she said that ...? Oh, yes—he'd been invited to join a softball team, but refused. She talked him into it, he sprained an ankle, and they teased each other for weeks about how she arranged it so he would be laid up at home with her.

"I suppose you're waiting patiently for me to continue. You were always a good listener." Logan realized he'd let his shoulders hunch, so he straightened up—she always hated the way he brooded when something bothered him.

"I already told you I met someone, when I came out that night and told you about the—the betrayal. Now I'm here ... now I'm here because someone told me to come."

He shook his head. "Dena, Maddie's assistant. You always told me to be open minded, but Dena's beyond belief, even by your standards. She told me ..." He chuckled, wondering that he should worry about someone who believed in spirits, when he held conversations with dead people. "She told me you were worried about me, and that the spirits watching over me were turning dark, and said I should come out here and talk to you."

"Which wouldn't bother me nearly so much, if not for the fact that I've never told anyone I come out here."

He sighed. "Coincidence? I don't know—you don't just guess something like that. Fate? Maybe Dena's an angel. There would be some irony there, since I practically accused her boss of being the devil. I was so certain, but now ... now I don't know."

So what was he out here for? He could hear Lise ask that, almost thought he did. He needed more than a sounding board.

"I guess I just want a sign, Lise. I always assumed you were up in Heaven, charming all the angels, but if you're here—or if some kind of spirit is keeping an eye on things—I need help. Some sign, something too coincidental to be a coincidence. I thought Maddie was the most wonderful woman I've met since ..." He paused, trying to control his voice. "Since you. Then I thought she was evil personified. Now—now I just don't know. Am I paranoid? Am I passing up a second chance at happiness? How do I know?"

For minutes he sat silently, head bowed, sometimes in prayer and sometimes in despair. He knew he couldn't give up the fight, no matter how much it put him into conflict with Maddie. He knew, also, that he was falling in love with her.

What he didn't know was how anything good could come from it. If there had ever been a chance between them, it would be lost the moment she walked into that Plan Commission meeting room. She would be lost.

Just as Logan started getting sore from being still for so long, a dull roar roused him. He glanced up in time to see, far in the distance, a truck clatter up the side road toward the cemetery. Few vehicles made enough noise to bother him up here, so he had no trouble recognizing Roy Mallie's white tow truck, and gazed at it without really seeing while his mind turned back to its own problems.

Then Logan jerked upright. The lumbering truck had been involved in an accident, apparently sideswiping a red vehicle. Paint had transferred to it, and some red lettering had been gouged off, changing the former sign, "Mallie's All Night Towing".

Now it read: "Maddie's All Right Too".

Logan watched until the truck disappeared, then listened until its growling motor faded into the distance. Then, very slowly, he got up and laid his hand on the tombstone before him.

"You always had an odd sense of humor, but … I get the idea. Thanks."

Maddie parked at the drive-in's entrance, hours before anyone would show up for the movies, and dodged under the swinging gate to get inside. She marveled at how different the place looked in midafternoon, brightly lit, with the rows of grassy knolls empty of vehicles.

There was a presence, though, and a sound. A riding lawn mower zipped around, and with a start Maddie recognized the drive-in owner, Martin Dunn, cutting the grass. She tried to picture one of the senior partners after closing hours, running a vacuum cleaner over the company's expensive carpet, and the image made her smile.

Dunn glanced up, paused for a moment, then turned the mower and roared toward her. Given everyone else's feelings, it seemed likely he planned to run over Maddie and bury the parts in the lot, but she squared her shoulders and marched forward.

When they were a row apart Dunn stopped the mower and climbed down, moving stiffly. "Well, Miss McKinley." He was well into his sixties and wore an old pair of slacks and a bright orange flowered shirt, along with a brimmed straw hat that protected his bald pate from the sun.

"Hello, Mr. Dunn. How did you recognize me?"

"I was sent a photo, courtesy the Chandler clan. Call me Marty." Much to her surprise, the old man gave her a hearty handshake and a welcoming smile. He was at least fifty pounds overweight, but had the animated expression of a much younger man. "I was warned you'd come around with a sales pitch, or threats."

Okay. There *was* something to be said for the time saved by not beating around the bush. "I'm surprised you weren't waiting with a shotgun."

"If I was upset about anything, it would be Tupper out organizing protests, instead of mowing the lawn like I pay him to. Besides, if Judy thinks you're a decent person that's good enough for me."

"Judy? Judy Chandler?" So Logan's mother had sneaked a photo of her. Of course, these people knew each other well—it wasn't like the big city, where a promise to get together was often an empty one.

"Judy's a wonderful judge of character." Dunn gestured for Maddie to follow him. "Come on, I'll show you around."

As they walked toward the concession stand, Dunn gave her a sidelong glance. "My grandfather bought this piece of ground, and built the drive-in fifty years ago, this month. My father helped him run it. When I retired from the factory after twenty-three years, I took over full time."

"Yes, I know." If Marty Dunn thought that story would get to her—he was right.

"I suppose you would. Now I'm sixty-five, and even though I get a little free time over the winter, sometimes I forget there's a life outside this place." He pointed to the big white house that bordered the property. "My grandfather built the house, too, and after dad died I moved in. It's too big, now that my wife has passed on."

Oh, boy. No wonder Dunn refused to consider giving up the

place.

Inside, Dunn showed her the cramped projection room and his office—about all there was, besides the concession area and bathrooms. The equipment had been updated at some point from speakers to an FM transmitted stereo sound system, then more recently to digital projectors. The whole place looked clean and in good repair, and Maddie didn't have to ask if the employees cared about their work.

After the tour they sat on folding chairs behind the concession counter, and Dunn looked around once more, with a sad frown. "Logan ... well, he thinks I'd be devastated to lose this place."

Maddie did too, but she steeled herself to make the argument she'd practiced on the drive over. "I know you love it, but—"

"I want out."

Maddie opened her mouth again, and it stayed open while her brain tried to process his words.

"It's not about money. We make a little profit, some years better than others. But I've worked hard, all my life—the military, the factory, here—and I promised my wife right up to the day she died that we'd stop soon and enjoy our retirement. For a long time afterward, there didn't seem any reason to give it up, but—" He noticed her expression and broke into a hearty laugh. "How do you like that? I made a lawyer speechless!"

"I just—you *want* to sell?"

Still grinning, Dunn shook his head. "Not to you, no offense. I do—to someone who will keep the drive-in open. I couldn't stand the thought of disappointing the locals, especially the young ones."

Maddie knew the feeling. "Logan kept talking about how terrible it would be for you—"

"I never told him how I felt. Why make him think I'm unhappy? The truth is, I want to travel, see the world while I can still enjoy it. But my kids moved out of state, and none are interested in the family business."

"Surely someone would be willing to take over—"

"No one with the capital to buy me out." Dunn's face clouded. "The only people with that kind of money plan to bulldoze the place, and to avoid that I'll stay and fight, whether I want to or not."

Maddie nodded, but her mind had already run away from the conversation. This was the crack her company needed, something they could exploit: Lean on a tired old man, throw money at him. Enough money for him to travel the world in style, for years to come.

But Logan didn't know about Dunn's dream. If he found out, he'd raise the cash to buy the old man out and run the drive-in himself, just to keep everyone happy. Dunn apparently didn't realize that, so everyone stayed in the dark.

Maddie's mind snapped back to attention. "How many people have you told about this?"

Dunn grinned. "Very few."

"Then why me?"

"Because you're one of the few people who actually has mixed feelings. You may change your mind, one way or the other, but the rest of us are fixed right where we are. You deserve to know everything."

Another voice broke in, from the end of the counter. "We both agreed on that, Maddie."

They looked up to see Judy Chandler, holding a picnic basket and a thermos. "I'm sorry, dear, I thought I'd be here when you arrived, but it seems you and Logan both managed to sneak out without my noticing."

"Your migraine—?"

"All gone. I thought I'd bring Marty some lunch, especially since I suspected you'd show up today."

Dunn stood, his smile widening, and offered Judy his chair. As she sat, he took the food from her, but set it aside and laid a gentle hand on her shoulder. She looked up, and their eyes met.

The flash that passed between them was all it took for Maddie to know these were more than two people fighting the same fight, or even two old friends. She also realized her situation had gotten much, much more complicated.

# CHAPTER NINE

"They're having an *affair*," Maddie wailed.

She steered the Porsche with both hands, letting go just long enough to yank at a loose strand of hair. Her hairstylist was the least of her problems, especially since she'd probably end up banned from ever approaching Boston again.

Dena didn't speak for so long Maddie thought she'd lost the Bluetooth connection. "Did you hear me? Logan's mother and the man I'm trying to drive to ruin are involved!"

"They told you this?"

"They didn't have to. Lawyers take an entire semester of reading body language."

"Sandwiched between 'Intro to Cheating 101' and 'Stealing for Fun and Profit', no doubt."

"This is serious, Dena. I ended up here because I mixed my personal and professional life, and now I'm more mixed up than ever."

"You can say that again. But have you considered this might be good news?"

"Right now the only good news would be if I spun off the road into a tree, and didn't have to face any of this." The thought made Maddie grip the wheel harder. "Plus, I got another run in my pantyhose from brushing the door when I left so quickly, and I only have two pairs left. Sheer Invites don't get runs. Do you have any idea how much—?"

"Okay, so how fast are you going?"

Maddie glanced down at the speedometer, then forced her foot away from the gas pedal.

"If you're not careful with that rocket ship you're piloting, you'll end up representing yourself—traffic court frowns on triple digit speeds."

"That's the least of my worries." Still, Maddie glanced into her rear view mirror, half expecting to see flashing lights. "So how could this possibly be good news?"

"If Marty and Judy are really in love—Marty and Judy, isn't that something?—they might be happy for the chance to run off together. In the end, maybe they'd be grateful to you."

"But Logan depends on his mother to take care of the children. Who would help him out?"

"Oh, I don't know—you?"

Maddie paused to control her car while she passed a semi, which also gave her a chance to catch her breath. She thought of spending her time with Faith and Conner and their all too sexy father, snuggled on the front porch with a glass of iced tea, or playing Frisbee in the back yard, or maybe helping plan a second chance wedding for the matriarch of the family—or her own wedding.

When did that suddenly become the ideal life?

"Maddie?"

"I'm here," she whispered, her voice almost carried away by the roar of traffic and wind.

"The Plan Commission may be ready to recommend rezoning the area—if all the property owners agree."

It took a moment for Dena's words to sink in. "How did that happen?"

"I got a phone call earlier from the Grand Rabid Bear in Boston. He says you're moving too slowly, and they're pursuing—and I quote—'other avenues'. Apparently that includes leaning on the Plan Commission members, but the only way they'll budge is if there's no question of using eminent domain for the airport. In other words, the area doesn't get rezoned unless the last holdout agrees to the plan."

"Marty," Maddie murmured.

"Marty's the center of the storm," Dena agreed. "One way or another they have to get him out of the way, and I'd rather it happen in a way that leaves him with something besides legal bills."

Maddie saw she was approaching her turnoff, and again took her foot off the gas. But her mind raced ahead, as she tried to find a way out of this dilemma that wouldn't leave somebody devastated. She'd already made her turn before realizing it was the wrong one. "Oh, no!"

"What is it?" Dena asked, reacting to the anguish in her boss' voice.

"I'm on a gravel road. This is going to ruin the Porsche's finish." The car fishtailed a little, and she reduced her speed more. "I'll have to have it repainted."

"Poor baby."

"I didn't even know they still had gravel roads in America." Maddie drove on, wincing at every ping of a stone against her car's undercarriage, until she found a turnoff that seemed to lead in the general direction of Hopewell. She was heartened to find the new road was paved, if bumpy. "This is where my whole life is going—into the choking dust of despair."

"You're breaking my heart," Dena told her, although Maddie could tell she was trying not to laugh.

"All right, fine. I'll have some meetings, if I ever work my way out of these corn fields. Maybe we can still find mutual ground."

"Sure, then we'll negotiate a Mideast peace treaty. Are you insane? The only difference between the firm of Quincy, Dixon, and Tremayne and a movie monster is that Godzilla left a few buildings standing."

"I'll—" Realizing there was no arguing with that truth, Maddie slapped the steering wheel. "Look, I'm almost there. We'll tackle this over a pot of coffee, all right?"

"I'll order up decaf from your archenemy—regular, no special blends."

Before Maddie could protest that they didn't need Logan's coffee—especially decaf—Dena hung up. They did need it, of course—with the shop downstairs, they'd never thought to buy a coffee maker. It seemed she needed Logan more and more every day, and not just for his shop's product. In fact, Heaven help her, not picking up the obligatory office coffee machine was probably a subconscious way to guarantee she would see him again, even if his next blend contained arsenic.

A moment later she reached the end of the pavement, where it crossed paths with another county road. Sure enough, she'd found her way out of the corn fields—ahead lay a bean field, which stretched away to a farm in the distance. "One high rise," she murmured, craning her head around. "Why couldn't Hopewell have one lousy high rise?"

A pickup truck rattled around the corner and stopped beside her. The man inside rolled down the window, giving both her and her car the once-over. "You lost?" He wore a green John Deere cap, and a suspicious bulge made his lower lip poke out.

"Hopewell?" A bow and arrows hung from a rack on the truck's back window, behind a bumper sticker that read, "My wife said I had to give up hunting; I'm gonna miss her." She reached for the door lock, as the theme from "Deliverance" played through her mind.

"Back that way." He pointed the way he'd come. "But be careful, old man Burkett's moving his combine down there aways, and there's not a lot of room to get around."

"Thank you very much." She drove on, before the man had a chance to spit on the Porsche's paint job. Sure enough, she had to maneuver around a huge farm implement, but when the farmer pulled over and waved her on she got by without a scratch. By the time she made it into Hopewell, the town seemed like a metropolis.

When Maddie pulled up to the curb, she saw the question of running into Logan was a moot point—he sat on the coffee shop's stoop, talking to a man who wore a black suit despite the warm afternoon sunlight. It looked like a full house inside, but from what Maddie could see through the front window, most of the customers were too busy craning their necks, and peering outside, to be demanding refills.

As she approached, the suited man nodded to her and disappeared into the jewelry store next door. Logan started bouncing a rubber ball on the sidewalk, and at first seemed not to notice her.

"Did you see?" he asked as she approached. "I broke my watch on a monument. I'll bet jewelers don't make house calls in the big city."

"On a monument?"

151

He glanced up. "It's a handball term. It means, um, the side wall."

"You should have taken your watch off." Is that what Dena whispered to him about? That he should go work off his frustrations with a handball game? That would explain why he seemed so much calmer, but not his reaction at the time.

Logan shrugged. "How did it go with Marty?"

She stopped in front of him, her insides lurching. "This *is* a small town, isn't it?"

"Mom called. Threatened me with bodily harm if you and I didn't kiss and make up." He leveled a hungry gaze on her lips, but kept catching the ball without looking at it.

Her memory of their last kiss burned so strongly that Maddie touched her lips, certain she'd felt his on hers again. "You knew Judy was out there?"

"She gets a lot of migraines—sneaks over there every few days, although I didn't realize it contributed to her 'headache' this time. She thinks nobody knows, but it's hard to be covert in a small town." He closed his fist around the ball, and gave her his full attention. "For instance, the whole county's wagging its collective tongue over calls Plan Commission members are getting."

"Yes, I just found out about that."

Logan stared at her, and Maddie realized without surprise that he was judging her honesty. "And?"

"And ..." Feeling dizzy, Maddie slumped down onto the step beside Logan. "And what do I do now? Give away possible strategies being worked out to use against you? Or keep my mouth shut and let all the people I've come to care for be hurt?"

Still examining her, Logan gave a sad smile. "On behalf of the whole town, I'm flattered that we sent you into an ethical tailspin."

"Yes, well—you're very handsome when you're challenging the foundations of my existence."

"And you're beautiful when you've having an anxiety attack."

"I never pictured building a relationship on that kind of emotional reaction." Not to mention, Maddie wasn't sure how honest she was being with him in non-legal areas. After all, Logan might know about his mother's visits with Martin Dunn, but was he aware it wasn't just friendship? She clutched her hands around her knees and sighed.

*Wait—"building a relationship"?*

"Want to get it off your chest?"

Maddie glanced at Logan, who grinned wickedly, then reached out to take her hand. "I mean that in a purely figurative sense."

"No you don't, or you wouldn't be smiling." But Maddie smiled too, and decided being up front with everyone was the only way to hold onto her self-respect. "The senior partners know small town groups like the Plan Commission tend to heed public opinion. In other words, veiled threats or bribes are a long shot. They'll still expect me to change minds, but from what I know of how Quincy, Dixon and Tremayne operates, I believe their calls to Commission members are a diversion."

Logan turned serious in a hurry. "So they plan dirty tricks elsewhere?"

Maddie nodded. "Which means I'm now part of the diversion, rather than the main plan, and at this point I'm not sure they trust me enough to tell me what's really going on. So you see, drilling me for—" She stopped when he grinned again. "That is, I'm out of the loop, and I've probably already slammed the brakes on my career. Chances are there's another associate, or even a partner, on the way out."

Logan squeezed her hand. "Then I guess you belong here with us now, Epiphany Girl."

"But I still—"

"I understand you have a job to do. But your heart is somewhere else, which makes all the difference." He leaned forward and pressed his lips lightly against hers, and Maddie couldn't help thinking that ruining her career was a small price to pay for another kiss from Logan Chandler.

The crowd inside the coffee shop broke into raucous cheering, and Maddie realized the door behind them was propped open. She felt her face redden as she looked back to see Logan's friends and customers applaud and whistle, while his children gave them twin thumbs up signs.

"You've gained their approval despite being an attorney," Logan announced, before planting another kiss on her cheek.

She turned to him, sensing a warmth she hadn't been able to welcome in a long, long time. "What was that, a community job interview?" She couldn't hold down her smile, but added, "I have half a mind to sue, if you set that up on purpose."

Logan held a protective hand up. "I plead innocent—granted, I was waiting for you to get back, but those reprobates in there must have opened the door and let all my air conditioning go free."

From inside, the same police officer Maddie had met her first time there called, "You want me to shoot somebody?"

While the next wave of laughter faded, Maddie's cell phone chirped. As soon as she answered, Dena whispered urgently, "You need to get up here."

"What is it? Partner trouble?" Maddie straightened, her mind racing. Although still relieved at the drop of tension between her and

Logan, she knew better than to think she would get through all this with her dignity intact, not to mention the risk to her job.

"You'd better believe it." Dena still whispered, as if afraid the room was bugged.

"I'm on the way." With a sigh, Maddie holstered the phone and stood, while Logan leaped to his feet beside her. "I have to go back to work—the demons are stirring."

"I'll walk you upstairs." Waving to his customers, Logan escorted her to the door next to his shop, which opened onto the inside stairway. "You know, it's not too late for you to just quit. In fact, we could use some legal help on our side."

She sighed again at the thought, and took his hand as they marched up the steps. "Contrary to popular belief, attorneys have ethical standards—"

"No. Really?"

"—Which include not switching sides in the middle of a case. I'll do their leg work for them."

At the top of the stairs Logan stopped, gripped her arms to turn her toward him, and kissed her, with far more desire than he'd shown in front of the crowd. She put her arms around him, parted her lips, and wished the moment would last at least until forever.

But all too soon he broke contact, then looked at her with another sad smile. "At least now you're not blindly charging down a path just because that's where you started."

"But I'm still the bad guy."

"I won't give up on you. Personally, or professionally." He turned her again, and gave her a gentle push toward the door. "Now, let's go in there and see what crisis the devil's own stirred up this time."

He followed her into the office, but bumped into her when she stopped short. Dena stood at the end of the hallway with a carafe of Logan's coffee, but Maddie saw only the man who sat ramrod straight in her chair, an ear to her phone while he punched, one handed, at her computer keyboard.

He looked up and grimaced, in what might have been an attempt at a welcoming smile, then spoke something unintelligible into the phone before hanging up. "Well, Madison—good afternoon." His Armani suit hung without a single wrinkle from his slim frame. Every thin, straw colored hair was carefully in place. When his green eyes flicked over to Logan they narrowed, and he pursed thin, bloodless lips.

"Welcome back from your field work. Is this an assistant?"

"This—this is Logan Chandler. I was discussing the case with him." Maddie felt breathless, and realized it was because she'd stopped breathing the moment she set eyes on the man.

"Good to see you're doing your job." He stood, took a step forward, and held his hand out toward Logan—a manicured hand Maddie knew all too well, one she couldn't believe she'd ever let touch her.

With a welcoming voice completely at odds with his expression, the man said, "How do you do. I'm Gilroy Tremayne—Maddie's fiancé."

# CHAPTER TEN

Logan couldn't remember ever taking such an instant dislike to anyone.

It wasn't just that Gilroy Tremayne had once been engaged to Maddie, although that seemed more than enough. It was the expression of superiority, the way he held his hand out with the clear assumption that he stood above anyone who took it.

Tremayne's eyebrow raised, as he gingerly shook Logan's hand. "Chandler—ah. The coffee person."

"Yeah." Logan squeezed, and got his reward when Tremayne's face paled. The local YMCA had good family membership deals, and a great weight room. "And you would be the East Coast lawyer with the bright ambitions and the dark soul."

Tremayne took a step back, and rubbed his hand. "I'm an agent of progress, Mr. Chandler."

"Is that so?" Maddie stared at her former fiancé, as if examining road kill. "Then why haven't you progressed to the point of realizing it's over between us?"

"Forgive me. Alluding to our former relationship is a bad habit I intend to change." Now his voice hardened, and Logan saw Maddie wince. "It is, indeed, over between us personally, and you're perilously close to it being over professionally, as well. The partners are disappointed that one of us had to dirty our hands with this, and I've seen nothing in your files to indicate we were wrong about your failures."

"You—" Maddie marched over to her computer and glanced at the screen, then whirled to face Tremayne again. "How did you get into my files?"

"Password 'Jordan'. Our personal relationship—former or not—remains an advantage."

The color drained from Maddie's face, and she dropped into her chair. Logan realized instantly that Jordan must be the name of Maddie's dead sister, and he was torn between going to her and punching the smug expression off Tremaine's mug. When Dana set the carafe down and hurried forward to put an arm around Maddie's shoulders, he made his decision and took one step toward Tremayne. The other man's words stopped him in his tracks.

"Your father was Ralph, correct?"

Logan clenched his fists. "What do you know about my father?"

"Born 1945. His parents were immigrants who started a bakery in Boston, then lost it to imminent domain in the fifties, when the city built a freeway through their neighborhood. They went bankrupt and he dropped out of school, spent some time in Vietnam with the army, then traveled to Indiana to help his parents start a new bakery, which became a coffee shop—this coffee shop."

Logan stared at him, his mind spinning with a thousand memories.

"Ralph Chandler married a woman he met here, continued to operate the shop after his parents died, fathered two sons and two daughters, then died of a heart attack five years ago. You, his first son, had two children after marrying—"

"Don't you dare even say her name, you son of a—"

Tremayne held a hand up, as calm as if discussing the weather in Japan. "I'm merely pointing out that I do my homework, Mr. Chandler."

"Those are just facts. Not people."

"It's not my job to know people." Tremayne turned away to look out the window, onto Main Street below. "It's my job to accomplish what my clients want, and in this case that's the construction of an airport." He waved his hands toward the window. "Those people don't matter."

"They matter to me."

"That's the point." He turned back, his gaze cold and hard. "You've been the greatest thorn in our side, so I made it my business to know everything about you, especially—" Now he turned a disapproving look toward Maddie. "Especially after you turned our best associate soft."

Logan also turned to Maddie, and saw her stricken look. Dena gripped her shoulders, but kept a murderous glare on Tremayne. "Go ahead and hit him, Logan."

"No!" Maddie straightened and caught Tremayne's eye, then looked away.

"No," Tremayne agreed, looking not the slightest bit worried. "That would suit me just fine, but it's not necessary. Events are progressing nicely, and Madison still works for us—she just wavered for a moment."

"I don't think so," Logan said.

But Tremayne smiled. "She's already read my new notes. Haven't you, Madison?"

Maddie glanced at the computer screen, then looked away. "Logan, why didn't you tell me what happened to your grandfather's bakery?"

Logan didn't answer, and the silence began to stretch until Maddie said, "That's why you hate lawyers, isn't it? I thought it started with the airport plan, but it's more than that."

"Yeah." Logan tried to clear the lump from his throat. "I didn't tell you because I thought it was history, but I guess I was wrong. I didn't realize ..." He faltered, seeing his grandfather again in the hospital, railing against the lawyers and politicians who took his home and business, and ruined his life. "I didn't realize it's always there."

Tremayne stepped forward again. Although he didn't make the mistake of placing a hand on Logan's shoulder, his voice became sympathetic, almost friendly. It made Logan all the more suspicious.

"I see no need to delve into personal issues. Yes, I could use this information against you, but why go there? We'll treat this purely as a professional issue—as long as you understand that Madison is to go back to work full time, and have no more contact with you."

"That's not gonna happen."

"Well, now, we must remember Madison has an ironclad contract with my company, including a no competition clause. If she left now, she'd be utterly unable to find work as an attorney anywhere in the nation. She wouldn't be able to afford to fight the lawsuit our firm would file against her for breach of contract, and she'd be most unhappy at being disbarred for unethical conduct."

"Unethical conduct?" Logan couldn't believe his ears. "All you people know about unethical conduct is how to hide it!"

"You don't consider working both sides to be unethical conduct?" Again, Tremayne held up his hand. "But really, shouldn't we let her decide?"

"Why don't we?" Logan turned to Maddie, but she didn't move at all. "Maddie?"

Slowly, as if with great effort, Maddie turned from the computer screen—but she couldn't meet his gaze. "I'm sorry, Logan. I have to complete my work with the firm."

"You—why?"

"I can't—we're in the middle of a legal process, I can't disclose …." Choking back a sob, Maddie shoved her chair back and ran into the corridor. A moment later they heard a door slam.

"You bastard." Dena pointed a shaking finger at Tremayne. "Someday I'll gouge out your eyes, then we'll see how well you keep that smug expression." She whirled, following Maddie.

Tremayne crossed his arms and smiled. "Emotional for a paralegal, isn't she?"

"I'm surprised you haven't had her beheaded." Logan stared at the other man, wondering what he was missing. Tremayne may have been engaged to Maddie, but Logan knew her—really knew her. He was tempted to march over and take a look at the computer screen, but he had a feeling he wouldn't like what it revealed.

Tremayne chuckled, still looking as if he'd been declared Emperor of the World. "She's pushing it. But Madison was very close to making junior partner, and we generally allow the junior partners to pick their own assistants. Besides, to remove her now would jeopardize my new deal with Madison."

"And what would that new deal be?" Keep talking, Logan told himself. Don't give in to the temptation to speak with your fists, not when so much remained unclear.

"She sees the project through, and in return we release her from her contract and give a fine recommendation. That's one of the notes on her screen—*our* screen."

What else was on the screen? Something involving blackmail, no doubt. A week ago Logan might have believed the worst about Maddie, but now he knew better. "So you brought her back in with threats, huh? How much damage can you do to her, to offset working for the devil?"

"Not just her." Now Tremayne's friendly smile became a warning sneer. "For now, Madison will be firmly in our camp until the ground breaking ceremony that will bring Quincy, Dixon and Tremayne into the lucrative Midwest property management business."

"Fine. You want a fight over property, I'll give you a fight. I'll fight for what I believe in, and unlike you, I'll fight fair." Then he leaned forward, to make sure Tremayne could see into his eyes. "Then we'll fight for Maddie, and I won't fight fair. Not at all. And I'll make sure if anyone gets hurt, it won't be her." He waited to make absolutely sure the other man knew who would be on the receiving end of the hurt, and when he saw the flash of fear in the lawyer's eyes he knew he'd succeeded.

"Well, then." Logan held out his hand. "To the end."

But Tremayne, unconsciously rubbing a hand still numb from the first handshake, refused the second one.

Maddie stood facing the little kitchen's sink, and didn't turn when the door behind her opened. She couldn't remember crying more than half a dozen times since graduating high school, but it took all her concentration to keep it from happening now.

But when Dena wrapped her arms around her waist and pulled her close, Maddie couldn't control it any longer. She turned around and sobbed on the smaller woman's shoulder, ashamed of herself, but glad to be with someone who understood.

It took only a few minutes for Maddie to gain control. Dena handed her a tissue, then a compact mirror, so she drew a ragged breath and set about repairing her makeup while her friend waited patiently.

When she finished, Maddie wondered at how calm and in control she looked. She handed the compact back to Dena. "I've lost him." Her voice quivered a little, so she tried again. "For good, this time." There—rock solid. Showing weakness to Gil was like slicing open an artery in shark infested waters.

"You haven't lost anything, yet." Dena told her with conviction.

"You saw the notes on the monitor. You saw what happened out there."

"Yes, but *he* saw what the senior partners are like. Logan's not the type to blame an employee when the owner is an ass."

"But ..." Maddie shook her head. For her entire life she'd followed a plan, step by step. She attacked all challenges and goals decisively, as she fought her way through college and law school, then worked her way up the ladder to—what? To become a partner. To be another Gil Tremayne.

But without that plan she felt like someone blindfolded, feeling their way through a maze with no idea of what dangers lay ahead. She realized that, since her sister's death, she'd spent every moment making sure no more surprises lay ahead. She'd succeeded. Up until her arrival in Indiana, there had been no surprises. No emergencies. No doubts.

No life.

"I am such an idiot."

"I believe I'm looking at someone having an epiphany." Dena examined Maddie's face. "Yes, I see a definite glow of discovery there."

Remembering she wasn't alone, Maddie turned to give her friend a hug. "That would be the second epiphany in one day. Fine—so my entire life has been a lie. I apologize for all those times I ignored your advice."

"About darn time. And I apologize for taking your car for a drive all those nights, while you were sleeping. So, now that you're ready to take a chance, will you try homemade beer, and skinny dip in the swimming pool?"

"Maybe to the beer. But I won't have a pool, or any clothes to wear, when the firm gets through with me." Everything Gil said was true: she couldn't leave the firm without serious consequences. "Also, I knew about the drives."

"So, you'll be a lawyer for underwear models. That way at least you'll still have some briefs." Dena gave her a wide smile, then glanced toward the door and sobered. "No, wait. Crapweasel in there is right, you can't just up and quit—especially since they'd just bring in another associate to do the dirty work."

"Crapweasel?"

"I feel a nickname makes him more approachable."

Maddie tried to smile. She couldn't imagine how to get Logan back, but maybe her place for the moment was right here, trying to ease the blow of whatever the firm planned. "We stay, then."

"For now," Dena agreed. "So, let's go get our marching orders."

"From Crapweasel." Maddie did manage to smile that time, but she sobered when they reached the end of the hallway and spotted Tremayne, cool as ever, as he hung up the phone.

He stood, shot them a triumphant smile, and began to pace the room while Maddie and Dena took their seats. "I just finished a strategy session with the main office, and our plan seems doable, if a bit unorthodox."

"A plan?" Maddie glanced at her computer screen and, with an irritated tap, sent Tremayne's notes to a hidden file. "You've given up on the idea of getting Martin—the drive-in owner—to sell?"

"Not exactly. Here's what we need." He punctuated each point with a finger. "Find out if the drive-in uses a sewer line."

Maddie shook her head. "Septic system."

"Excellent. Find out how old it is. I need an estimate on the average number of vehicles parked there per night since he started operations. I need to know who their trash hauler is, and whether they use recycling or have any special arrangements for hazardous waste."

Maddie and Dena exchanged puzzled looks.

"I need to know the soil type under the drive-in, and how much of the surface is gravel or dirt, compared to grass. Find out about the water table, and which direction rainwater drains from the property. And—" He looked around with a satisfied grin. "I need some furniture for my office, something bigger than these desks. Oak, I think."

"What are you planning?" Maddie demanded, although the awful answer had already presented itself to her.

"To furnish my office, of course. This job could take weeks." He eyed her legs. "You'll need to replace those snagged pantyhose if you're going out in public on company business."

"You know what I mean, Gil. What about the property? What have you figured out that I didn't?"

"You actually gave me the idea, Madison, by making one too many comments about playing dirty." Tremayne perched on a folding chair and crossed his legs, his smile widening. "I'm going to bring dirt into this, literally. I'm going to have the drive-in declared a brown zone."

Dena gave a horrified start. If the drive-in was declared contaminated it would be closed immediately, leaving the owner responsible for the cost of cleaning it. Marty Dunn would be financially ruined, bankrupt—no retirement fund, no world travel, no comfortable cruises with Judy on his arm.

Maddie stood, trying to keep her voice level, trying not to show how sick she felt. "Gil, it doesn't have to be like that. We've only just begun talks with Dunn. A higher offer, and he might still sell—"

"We're done talking," Tremayne snarled, his pleasant attitude vanishing. "You had your chance to do it your way. Now you'd better toe the line if you want to save yourself."

Maddie cast around desperately for something, anything, that would save Marty. "If that ground is declared contaminated, no one will be able to use it. Not for a drive-in, not for an airport."

Now Tremayne smiled again, but it was a nasty, victorious smile. "Oh, the development company will gladly pay the cost of cleanup, as a community service. Tax write-off. But first, of course, Mr. Dunn will have to give us the property. At a much, much lower cost."

"You're a monster."

"Maybe." Tremayne stood and came toward her, until his narrow face was inches away. "But you'll help this monster, won't you? Not just for your job."

Maddie held her breath, as if breathing in his scent would contaminate her. "I read the note."

"Then you know why you have to change some opinions at the Plan Commission meeting. You know about the field the firm bought,

166

north of here. You know about the platted road that runs right through one corner of a certain cemetery. You know that, with the signing of a few papers, I can have the road developed, and that would require moving some graves. And you know what would happen then:

"We'll dig up Logan Chandler's wife and father."

Logan tried to sneak into the shop's back room, but just as he reached a stealthy hand out, Lydia slapped it away. "What are you doing? Get away from my cookies!"

"Sorry," he said, rubbing his hand. So much for a snack, and he'd just started getting his appetite back.

"What are you doing here, anyway? It's nearly suppertime." Lydia bustled around the room, cleaning up from her last batch of baking.

"Mom took the kids out for supper, so I'm a free agent."

"That doesn't mean you shouldn't have a good meal—" She stopped and twisted around, giving Logan a narrow look. "It's that new lawyer, isn't it? You don't want to leave them alone in the building."

Logan, who had just started for a cookie again, froze in mid-reach. "Well ... they might break in here and take all your dough."

"Oh, for Heaven's sake. Dena was down earlier, telling me this fellow gives off bad vibes—doesn't he have any good qualities?"

"He has this neat trick where he hides olives in his nose." Giving Lydia a defiant look, he gobbled down a cookie before she could protest. But he didn't reach for another—talking about Tremayne took his appetite again.

The older woman glared at him, hands on hips, but before she could say anything the double doors swung open. Maddie stepped in, a carafe in her hand, and locked eyes with Logan.

"And what do *you* think of Mr. Tremayne?" Lydia asked.

"He's a boil on the butt of humanity." Maddie's gaze didn't waver. "The girl at the counter said I could come through."

"For more coffee?" Lydia grabbed the carafe and, without another word, bustled through the door.

"I didn't come for coffee," Maddie said, still staring at Logan. "That was just the excuse."

"She knows." God, she was beautiful. Her eyes were a bit red, and she'd used a pencil to pin back her hair, and her lipstick had faded away at some point in the afternoon. And she was beautiful.

"I've been thinking a lot about your wife, and your father." Finally she looked away, toward the floor. "They must have been wonderful people, for you to have loved them so much."

The way she said it seemed strange. Strained, as if she was trying to tell him something, but couldn't get the words out. "They were. Sometimes they didn't realize how wonderful they were—which brings us to the present, and to you. I don't think you have any idea how amazing you are."

Without another word, Maddie threw herself forward and crashed into him. Their lips met, and he felt her hands roam over his body for just a second, before they settled around his waist to pull him closer. Logan wrapped his own arms around her shoulders and rejoiced in her taste, her smell, the warmth of her skin.

All too soon, she pulled away. "I can't stay. He'll get suspicious."

"You make it sound like we're having an affair."

"We are. I'm cheating on my work." She pressed her lips to him again, then spun away and headed back out. "Thanks ... for the coffee."

"Wait." She paused while he took another carafe from the counter and filled it halfway with decaf. Then he rummaged through a cupboard, coming out with a handful of ingredients that he doled generously into the coffee. He closed the lid, swirled the carafe to mix the concoction, and handed it to Maddie. "When you use coffee as an excuse to come down here, you have to go back with something to show for it. Here's a new blend, in honor of our VIP upstairs. A special blend."

She took it gingerly, as if it might bite. "And what do you call this?"

He smiled. "I call it ... The Mexican Jumping Blend. Make sure he gets it. You might want to avoid pouring it into Styrofoam cups. You might also want to avoid being in front of him when he takes a sip."

"Got it." She leaned forward, leaving one last kiss on the edge of his mouth, then headed back for the door. "Thanks again."

"My pleasure." It was all he could do not to pull her into the storeroom, lock the door behind them, and make her forget all about Tremayne or anything else.

At the exit she turned back again, with a strange, wistful look that contained only half a smile. "You taste like chocolate chips." And she was gone.

Logan stared after her, head spinning. After a moment he tugged at his shirt, trying to pull himself together, and that was when he felt the rustle of paper in his hip pocket. He pulled the note out and read it twice. His mood spiraled downward, and he almost didn't notice Lydia come back in.

"Well, was she—what's wrong?" He forced his gaze up, and found

169

Lydia staring at him with an alarmed expression.

"It's—nothing."

"Oh, yes it is."

"It's—I have to go." He could feel the rage building up, swelling within him, as if all his years of control had just made it stronger. Before he could lash out at someone who didn't deserve it, he rushed through the door.

Logan saw nothing but a wash of red as he stalked down the street, fists clenched, and his mood hadn't improved by the time he used his key to sneak into the basement of the Lutheran Church on Third Street. The weight room down there, part of the church's outreach to young people, was more private than the YMCA. It was also roomier and brighter than the basement corner at home, where a few odd pieces of fitness equipment waited.

Besides, he'd torn open his own punching bag the night he found out why Maddie came to Indiana.

Now Logan needed something else to beat up on, something that wouldn't land him in jail. The crumpled note rustled in his hip pocket, a note in Maddie's crisp, elegant hand writing, so un-lawyerlike, but full of lawyerlike words. Brown field. Contamination. He didn't know how Maddie managed to sneak it by Gilroy Tremayne, but knowing what that jerk planned didn't give him any ideas about how to prevent it.

He really, really needed to beat up on something.

Without changing or warming up, Logan attacked the church's punching bag, hitting and kicking with all four limbs, aiming for the spot where his mind placed Tremayne's head. Sweat rolled down his face, soaking his shirt, but he went on. His muscles began to cramp, but he went on. His knuckles ached, then went numb, but he went on.

He didn't know how much time passed before he collapsed,

hugging the bag to keep from falling to the floor. His breathing had just begun to ease when a low, powerful voice cut through his dark thoughts.

"The Lord sent me. He said you've smited enough."

A man Logan's age watched him from the doorway. He wore close cut black hair, a carefully trimmed beard, and a white collar that topped his dark outfit. "I'm guessing you've been trying to keep yourself from breaking the jawbone of an ass?"

"Very funny, Jake."

Jake grasped his wheelchair and rolled into the room, stopping by Logan. "It's okay, I can make Biblical jokes. It's like redneck jokes— they're not as offensive if a redneck makes them."

Logan sank to the floor, letting the punching bag swing into his back. "Yeah, but rednecks are funnier."

"It's the accent. I took a class in Biblical humor, by the way—it helps break the tension. Have you noticed some tension, my son?"

"Forgive me father, for I badly want to sin." Logan looked away.

"We're Lutheran—just tell me what's on your mind."

"I've fallen in love with a lawyer."

"Shocking, but old news, my friend."

"I just met her ex-fiancé. He's a blood sucking lawyer. I mean, he actually has fangs and everything." He told Jake the story of their meeting, then waited while the pastor tilted his head and thought about it.

"So you've been hurt by her secrets, then by her refusal to switch sides, but you still love her."

"Since the moment she walked through the concession stand door, but I didn't realize it then." Logan drew a long, ragged breath. "Earlier today ... today's the day I knew."

"Well, you have to figure out who to forgive."

"What?"

Jake grinned at him. "We've had this discussion before, Logan. Blame gets spread all over the place, especially in cases of personal injury."

"Wait a minute—the whole reason you caught me down here is because I'm trying to avoid doing personal injury."

"I said personal, not physical. Look, when you got thrown into the back of a police car it all seemed cut and dried. Someone hit your teammate. You hit them. I blamed him for a while, and you never stopped. The truth is, all that blame made no difference at all—I was still in this wheelchair, which could just as easily have happened to the fellow you assaulted."

Again, Logan looked away, but Jake reached out and pulled on his shoulder until he had to turn back again. "First you have to figure out where all the blame is going—only then can you work toward forgiveness."

"Oh, come on." Standing, Logan punched the bag again, then walked away to stand by the far wall. "You're a Hoosier, man—just come straight out and tell me what you're trying to tell me."

But Jake shook his head. "That's cheating, and I think it'll be better if you work it out for yourself. All I'm going to tell you is this—you need to settle your past before you can go on into the future."

"That's ridiculous. I've put everything behind me."

"Have you? Then why do you still have all this rage?"

172

"You didn't meet the guy."

Settling back, Jake shook his head. "He's the only reason you removed all the skin from your knuckles? No, he's just the trigger. Is there anything else you want to tell me?"

"What, you took classes in psychology, too?"

"As a matter of fact, I did." Crossing his arms, Jake waited.

Logan stared at him, but the surge of adrenaline had drained away, along with the strength necessary to keep secrets. He finally slid down the wall to a sitting position, then bowed his head. "I go to the cemetery. I talk to Lise."

"Of course you do."

Logan whipped his head up, so rapidly his neck protested with a sharp pain. "This doesn't surprise you?"

"Why should it? It's a natural part of the healing process, and just because time's passed doesn't mean you've healed. I do question why you bother going to the cemetery, though."

"Well, I ..."

"She'll listen wherever you are, as long as you need her to. Then, one day, you'll move on, and she'll know she can rest easy."

"When you became my spiritual adviser, I didn't know we'd end up actually discussing spirits." He thought of Dena, and shivered a little.

"A lot of things in this world we don't understand, and aren't meant to. But there's one thing I do understand, and that's love." Jake wheeled forward again, so he could reach out and grip Logan's shoulder. "You love this woman, any fool can see that."

"Including you?"

Grinning, Jake slapped him on the back. "I see your face when you talk about her. I think you can overcome your differences, and you might even learn to get along with that ex-fiancé."

"Before you say that, there's something else. A note Maddie slipped to me." He reached into his pocket for the crumpled paper, and handed it over. "This is the trigger."

Jake read it through twice, just as Logan had, then stared off into space for a long moment before turning back to his friend. "Logan, what I'm about to say, I'm saying in a purely figurative way. Understand?"

Logan nodded.

"Kick his ass."

# CHAPTER ELEVEN

"I'm me again," Maddie said.

Dena, standing behind her as they gazed into the hotel room's full length mirror, drew a heavy sigh. "You are, indeed."

Maddie's new million dollar hairstyle, artfully designed to cascade down her back in loose ringlets but not get in the way if she bent over paperwork or a computer keyboard, screamed Professional Woman. Lightly applied makeup contrasted enough to make her features visible to a room full of listeners. Her dress, burgundy with a white collar, wasn't too severe, but featured a high enough neckline to avoid distracting anyone. With a hem just above the knees, it resembled something from the 50s.

Maddie had plenty of experience dressing for these meetings. It was her face she studied, her expression. There it was, back where it belonged: The cool, aloof, professional detachment. It went missing when she took that shameful dive from the professional to the personal. Now, after a whole weekend of conference calls to the office and the development firm, and hours spent pouring over dry, detailed paperwork, she'd found it again.

The expression of a woman who would never sit holding hands at the drive-in.

Something squeezed her chest for a moment, but she turned away from it and her image, to look at her assistant. Dena had tied her hair back in a long black ponytail, and wore a pink silk dress that struck Maddie as being off balance because it featured a mid-thigh hemline and long sleeves. It was as close to conservative as she'd ever seen on her friend.

Dena also wore a dour expression.

"This is our job," Maddie reminded her. "We're doing what we're paid to do."

"So we're just following orders?"

Maddie's vision turned red for an instant, while she fought to keep her famous coolness. "Dena, if we can't convince Marty Dunn and the Plan Commission at this meeting, the firm will have his property condemned and he'll lose everything. You know that." She never lost her temper with Dena, even in the worst possible moments. What the devil was wrong with her?

"And they could dig up the Chandler family plot—yeah, I know. We work for people who would do something like that."

But Dena—Dena always wore her heart on her sleeve. "Deenie, maybe you should stay here."

The other woman's eyes widened. "What?"

"This'll be a rough meeting, and I'll emerge as public enemy number one. If you're with me, you'll be guilty by association. If you're not, there may still be some good will toward you that we can use later."

Dena considered it for a moment, then turned to pick up Maddie's black briefcase. "You may not realize it yet, but you need the moral support. You also may need me to watch your back on the way out the door. So let's go."

Without another word, Maddie turned toward the door. She wanted to show her gratitude, but dared not reveal any emotion at all, when it had taken her all weekend to bring that unreliable self-control back. Anyway, Dena knew her well enough that some things didn't need to be said.

The bank clock down the street read 5:30, but the sun still stood high in the sky as the two women walked out to the Porsche. It was hot, in the mid-eighties, which wouldn't help when tempers began to flare. Maddie began to hope against hope that something—softball games, air conditioned homes, anything—would keep people away from the City Hall tonight.

As Maddie pulled into traffic, Dena asked, "So what did you tell Logan?"

Maddie gripped the steering wheel until she thought it would break. "I found a speeding ticket in the glove compartment. How many laws did you break getting my Porsche here from Boston?"

"Don't change the subject, counselor."

"I thought we weren't going to discuss him." Maddie forced her grip to loosen, and flexed her fingers to get the blood flowing again.

"I'm dying, here."

"I haven't told him anything. I suspect he thinks I refused to go to the meeting … he'll know otherwise in a few minutes."

Dena pulled on a pair of sunglasses. "Can hardly wait."

Maddie's throat constricted at the thought, but nothing more could be done. Soon he would know the facts, and facts were stubborn things.

Vehicles lined both sides of Main Street for two blocks in either direction from the City Hall. Maddie drove by twice, coolly sizing up the cars, pickups, and vans. She took note of the drive-in bumper stickers, and a crowd of young people congregated at the nearby library while their parents attended the meeting. These were families, not corporate reps—her two greatest enemies would be roots and tradition.

Dena didn't bother to hide her dismay. As they walked the three blocks from the nearest open parking spot, she glanced around as if searching for snipers. "Suppose they have tar and feathers? What if they don't put us near the exit, and we can't get out before somebody brings a rope?"

Maddie stopped in front of an old, ornate set of wooden doors and looked at her friend. "This is Indiana. Gentlemen don't hit women, and nobody's been lynched here since 1930. I checked." She turned to pull open a door, then marched through a short hallway and yanked open a second set of doors.

An entire room full of people turned grim, expectant glares at the new arrivals.

Behind her, Dena whispered, "Did you really research that lynching thing, or was it an educated guess?"

The lawyer in her told Maddie she could get the whole meeting shut down for fire code violations. Perhaps two hundred people had jammed into a wood panel lined room meant for half that, which left all the seats full and a layer of bodies pressed against three walls. The last wall, at the front of the room, held a long table behind which sat the Plan Commission members, while in the row before them various public officials filled all but a few empty seats.

She saw Logan instantly. Looking sharp in tan slacks and a navy button up shirt, he had stationed himself close to the door to greet friends and neighbors as they came in. Now he looked up, did a double take, and started to smile.

Then he glimpsed her briefcase, saw her expression, and faltered.

"You're not here to offer support, are you?" When she shook her head, he leaned in to whisper, "I got your note. You know what they're—"

"I'm trying to stop that."

"This isn't the way."

"It'll leave him with something." She wanted to apologize again, but it would be far too easy to fall at his feet, beg forgiveness, and abandon all she'd worked her entire life for. Instead she squared her shoulders and glanced pointedly around at the people closest to them, who murmured, depending on whether they'd met her, in surprise or shock. "The meeting's about to start. This isn't the time to discuss … mistakes."

With considerable effort, Logan unclenched his fists and took a deep breath. "I already know what mistake *I* made." He stood to one side of the narrow corridor between seats, and waved her forward with a show of politeness too stiff to be believed.

The Plan Commission President waited until Maddie and Dena were seated before he went through the typical meeting opening procedures, then paused to sweep a warning look over the audience. "This is a preliminary hearing, and public comments will not be taken tonight. If there are any outbursts, the room will be emptied— understood? We'll hear two presentations tonight on the proposal to rezone an area within Hopewell's two-mile zoning area from Agricultural to Industrial One. The first is from Madison McKinley of Quincy, Dixon and Tremayne, which represents the development company, and the second from Logan Chandler, representing the organization—Logan, what are you calling your organization?"

Logan, who had sunk into a chair to Maddie's left, started. Clearly he hadn't considered naming the antidevelopment group, which meant it wasn't well organized. That boded well for Maddie's efforts, which didn't cheer her up in the least.

Someone in the back called out, "No New Noisy Neighbors", which brought a laugh from the crowd and a bang from the President's gavel. After a moment Logan stirred and cleared his throat.

"Friends ... Friends for the Future." That brought a ripple of approval.

"Very well." The President nodded to Maddie. "Miss McKinley? You're up."

As she stood, Maddie glanced with understanding at Dena—it did indeed feel like she'd been called to her execution. Dena started to open the briefcase, but Maddie shook her head, having already memorized the notes inside.

She stood by a large map hung beside the Plan Commission table, which showed the town and an outline of the proposed area to be rezoned. It was divided by property owner, and a small square near the center represented the drive-in.

"A local developer, based in Fort Wayne, is offering your community a unique opportunity for economic growth. The regional airport they propose will be an advanced and modern facility, which might eventually replace Smith Field as the primary backup airport for Fort Wayne International."

As she spoke, Maddie scanned the crowd and saw many familiar faces, but not one hint of hospitality. "This would be a direct way for residents of this area to catch local flights, instead of having to make an hour long drive to reach the other side of Fort Wayne."

Nothing. Clearly, these people couldn't care less about air travel in northeast Indiana, so she switched to the big guns in the hope of opening their minds.

"What's in it for you? The project would bring well paying, professional jobs and an influx of much needed cash to your community, without a major hit on resources. Our studies indicate most of those who would use the airport would come from the south, so your traffic patterns would not be adversely affected. At the same time, there will be an increased demand for housing and support services, which will allow the town of Hopewell to grow in a controlled manner and—more importantly—give your youth a chance to take advantage of the opportunities that might keep them here."

A face near the back of the crowd caught Maddie's attention, and she faltered despite herself: Logan's mother, dabbing at her eye with a handkerchief.

"I understand your concerns, especially about losing the drive-in." She spoke now directly to the Chandler family. "I've been there. I enjoyed myself, and made—friends. But compare the loss of one small business to the good our proposal will do for your entire community."

This wasn't right—she sounded desperate. A slight pause allowed her to gather herself without giving someone else a chance to spout off. "The proposal will broaden your tax base considerably. It gives you the opportunity to modernize and expand city services without a comparable tax increase. Best of all, it brings the possibility that your children, the same bright people who would someday flee to better prospects elsewhere, will have a future right here with their friends and family."

Maddie continued with statistics about Indiana's "brain drain". She spoke for another fifteen minutes, into a silence so deep she caught herself wondering if she'd suddenly gone deaf. Her audience might as well be deaf, for all they listened to her, and she took her seat knowing her carefully prepared and compelling arguments might as well be gibberish.

The Plan Commission President nodded to Logan. "Mr. Chandler, do you have a response?"

"I certainly do." Logan stood and strode to the same position

Maddie had held, by the map. His gaze swept the room, hesitating only an instant as their eyes met. "Miss McKinley spoke of what good could come from replacing woods, and swamps, and fallow fields, and a drive-in with a regional airport. She said our economy would improve, and our children benefit."

He paused, with a dramatic flair that surprised Maddie. "She's absolutely right."

The onlookers gave a universal gasp.

"A community must, indeed, grow to live. We all know of ghost towns scattered around this area, towns that shriveled and died on the vine because they didn't grow. We do have a brain drain in Indiana. We need opportunities, challenges, *reasons* for our children to stay."

He paced before the Plan Commission members, who looked puzzled as Logan seemed to argue against his own position. "I'm a local businessman. I would benefit from more housing, more jobs. It would give me more customers and leave my small business secure and prospering. Then we could all sit in the coffee shop, look out over our bustling community…"

Again he paused, his steady gaze sweeping over the hushed crowd. "And watch our city go to hell."

The people erupted: cheered, clapped, whistled and stomped. It took a good five minutes of gavel pounding for the President to bring order, while Logan stood quietly before the map. Then, just as he could be heard again, Logan raised his arm and pointed an accusing finger right at Maddie.

"She doesn't live here."

Maddie heard Dena gasp, but couldn't look away from Logan and his burning, accusing gaze.

"Not a single executive in the development company, or that

group of lawyers that represents them, lives here."

Logan dropped his arm and again addressed the whole crowd. "This isn't about bottom lines. It's not about numbers. This is about people. If the airport is built, we'll gain numerous jobs at the expense of one small business, barely a speck on this map. The lawyers would tell that you only this man, and his handful of part time employees, would suffer."

Logan pointed to Marty Dunn, who hunched his shoulders and stared at the floor. His great belly strained against his gray suit in a way that made it obvious it had been in the closet for some time.

"For fifty years his family ran a drive-in theater among the fields and woods near our town. For fifty years it's been an institution, but it's not a huge financial success. It could disappear in an instant without a blip on our economic radar.

"What it is, is ours. How many of us played there as kids? How many watched our first movie, worked our first part time job, kissed our first love there?" Logan faltered for an almost undetectable moment. "How many of us had grandparents who watched Jerry Lewis comedies there, and how many of us now take our children?"

He looked again at Maddie, with the same expression he might have after stepping into a dog pile.

"I will never accept that money is more important than people. A town may grow, but if it doesn't keep its character it's just as dead as a little crossroads with an empty church and a boarded up general store. Character means a place to take your family, a place that will become special to every generation. The drive-in is more than a parking lot where you can watch movies: It's a beloved part of our community, and no slab of concrete runway will ever replace it."

The applause grew louder this time, and longer, and for all the lack of concrete benefit in Logan's argument, Maddie knew he'd won this round. She wondered if he headlined his college debate team.

He had to hold a hand up to quiet the audience, and when they grew silent again continued. "Kids can't play at an airport. They can't form beloved childhood memories over a glass control tower. They can't come to love their friends and family and neighbors in a terminal. No bar graph, no statistical analysis will ever replace what that little grassy field with the big silver screen gives Hopewell. We will never—ever—give up, we will never stop fighting, until those outsiders take their greed and build their airport somewhere else." Without waiting for a response, he spared Maddie one more glare and took his seat.

Only he, Maddie, and Dena remained seated. A deafening roar slammed off the walls as everyone cheered, yelled, and reached out to slap their hero on the back. No Plan Commission member even tried to call for quiet.

Maddie couldn't blame them. Heaven help her, she even agreed with him. From this point on, no matter how this project ended, she knew it would end badly for her.

# CHAPTER TWELVE

Just after dawn the next day, Logan settled down on his bench and cast his eyes over the cemetery. This time of year, daybreak came too early for anyone to be around, and he had the whole world to himself—just as he preferred it when he came here.

"Good morning, Lise."

The tops of pines and oaks, scattered around the cemetery, glowed in the first rays of sunlight, while fog lay in low spots and shrouded the field behind him. The day promised to be warm, but right now, with the exception of the dew that soaked through the seat of his pants, he couldn't imagine being more comfortable. Physically comfortable, anyway.

"I forgot to bring a towel for the bench, Lise. I'll bet you get a big kick out of that."

The dark granite headstone could give no reply. Only a bird answered, suddenly chirping away as if surprised to find it morning already.

"Why do things have to be so complicated?"

With a sigh, he threw his arms over the back of the bench. Things had always been complicated, really. Running a business, raising a family, dealing with his father's death and his wife's ... even his

185

relationship with her wasn't as easy as his rose colored memories made it seem. After all, he fell in love with Lisette at one of the lowest points in his life, when she saved him from his self-loathing after he attacked the teen football player who crippled Jake.

"Jake says hello. I finally told him I've been talking to you, and he thought it was the most natural thing in the world. Of course, being a man of the cloth, he knows you're listening. So do I."

He closed his eyes, and memories blurred together, all of them set in the same hospital. Jake, Lise, his father, all hooked up to tubes and monitors, all watched over by one man who—

Logan's eyes snapped open. "I blamed myself."

How could he have not seen it earlier? No wonder he had such an attraction to Maddie. Birds of a feather. Each blamed themselves for the deaths of loved ones, even when it wasn't their fault.

He whispered into the silence. "For Dad, and you, even Jake—like I was cursed somehow. Oh, Lise. You and Jake pulled me out of that first funk, but I disrespected you by not forgiving myself, not seeing how blessed I was. Now Maddie's come along, and I almost threw her away, too. That's what Jake was trying to tell me."

He hung his head for what seemed a long time, until he realized if anyone saw him they would think he was grieving. Straightening, he looked around, prepared to explain he was giving thanks. The high points of the cemetery now lay fully in the sunlight, as fog began to fade from the valleys, but he still saw no one.

"When Maddie came down for coffee last night she told me she'd been thinking of you and dad. I don't know why. I think she wanted to tell me something else, but ... anyway, I took it as a sign that I should stop down."

He waited, then gave an embarrassed chuckle. "Not that I couldn't

186

talk to you anywhere. But this place has nice ambiance, and the tenants keep it quiet as a tomb."

Logan paused again, almost expecting one of the cemetery's occupants to protest.

"She slipped me a note. Tremayne wants to have the drive-in declared contaminated, and if that happens Marty will lose everything. The community will lose, all of us will, but especially Marty.

"I still don't know what to do. While everyone else sleeps I sit here, trying to figure out how to handle this David and Goliath thing I've gotten myself into. I know we're right. I know we're fighting the good fight. But how do we win?"

He paused, watching squirrels and rabbits work their timid way across the ground before him.

"Another sign would be nice."

That's when he heard the music. The timing sent a shiver up his spine, but when he concentrated he realized it had been with him for some time, faint and almost swallowed by the heavy, humid air. Flutes, strings, and drums, combined into some kind of dance music. He cocked his head, trying to locate the source, then craned his neck to look past the fence into the field behind him.

He almost fell off the bench.

A figure emerged from the wisps of fog. It danced in knee high grass, twirled and jumped as if on stage, in perfect time to the music. At first Logan thought it was a child, waifish but athletic, like a gymnast. She wore a dress of pastel layers, which flowed around her as she leaped and spun until she seemed like a flower, dancing in the wind. Her hair, jet black and waist length, added to the effect as it flowed with her movements.

When the music faded she slowed, then stopped in a position of coiled strength, ready to spring at the first notes of the next piece. But before she could take off again, she glanced his way and smiled, her brown eyes dancing.

Mouth open, Logan rose to his feet. "Dena?"

Maddie's assistant stepped toward him, but didn't speak as she caught her breath. Her outfit, he realized, consisted of some kind of a dance costume, a multicolored leotard, blue tights and light skirt. He also noticed, hanging from a rawhide string around her narrow waist, a rabbit skin pouch that didn't match the rest of the outfit.

She noticed him staring at it, and laid a finger on the small pouch. "It's a traditional medicine bag from my great-grandfather's tribe. He gave it to me when I went to college."

"That was an incredible dance."

"The dance was also traditional, but I gave it a little update." She stopped short of the waist high wire fence that divided the field from the cemetery.

"Not a rain dance, I hope."

"A dance of hope and faith." Dena gave an embarrassed shrug. "The music—not so traditional. At least, not for my ancestors."

"It all fit. Do you come here often?" Realizing how that sounded, Logan mentally kicked himself.

Dena just laughed. "No. My great-grandfather taught me to dance at his home—although I put a little more flow into it—and then I taught dance in Boston. But this is the first time since we came here ..." She paused, her face darkening as if she'd remembered something dancing had removed from her mind. "Anyway, I felt the need to commune with the spirits a bit, and what better place than a graveyard?"

"But you're not actually *in* the graveyard."

"I'd trip over the headstones." She grabbed a fence post, and before Logan could offer to help, scrambled over. He noticed she wore blue slippers, now soaked with dew. "There's nothing like this in Boston. Parks, yes, but they all seem sterile, too planned ... the air even smells different. I love it here. For two cents, I'd sink in my roots and never go back to the coast."

"Maybe so, but whoever owns that field might frown on your dancing around in it."

Dena looked away. "It's owned by a farmer who lives a few miles from here."

"How do you know that?"

"We have the records, because the firm has an option to buy the property."

"The firm—" Logan's vision blurred as he processed the news. He pictured a high rise, topped by a heliport, casting noise and shadow over Lise, his father, and everyone else laid to rest at this quiet spot. "Why?"

"Blackmail." Dena stepped into the Chandler family plot, then paused to read each name on the few headstones there. "Back in the sixties, developers platted this area as a housing development, but then a recession hit and nothing ever got built. The cemetery expanded a little that way, but no official zoning or ownership change was ever made to account for it, so technically it was illegal."

"What are you saying?"

Dena raised her hands to encompass every stone in the plot, and other graves along the fence. "They platted a street, right here, to access the north side of the development. Quincy, Dixon and Tremayne are going to go into the development business themselves,

189

and put a nice residential addition—" She stepped over to rap her knuckles on the bench "—right here. If ..."

Logan stared at her, struggling to catch his breath. "If? If what?"

"If Maddie doesn't do her job." Dena sank onto the bench, and after a moment Logan sat beside her. They stayed silent, until the imagined sound of bulldozers became too much for him.

So that was why Maddie did her best to beat him at that Plan Commission meeting. If Dunn gave in and sold the property outright, he'd come out with a profit—and the Chandler family plot would be safe. "That was one of the notes on the computer screen, wasn't it? A threat?"

"No threat. Just a press release announcing the location of a new, upscale housing addition. Gil Tremayne is very careful about how he words anything that might become public."

"Tremayne." Logan turned the name into a curse word.

"I like to call him Crapweasel. It makes me feel better, somehow. But that's the only thing that's made me feel better, because I haven't been able to get anything to pin on him."

"You're trying to pin something on him?" On second thought, Logan wasn't at all surprised.

"Yeah, ever since he started getting touchy-feely while Maddie was gone the other day." Dena shrugged. "I'm too low on the totem pole for a relationship, but now that he's given up on Maddie he's looking for another conquest. I haven't been able to pin *that* on him yet, either."

"Good Lord. Should I—?"

"I can take care of myself. But he's careful—he'd never be inappropriate where there might be witnesses. That's how he is on the job, too: Like if he has to keep any incriminating notes, he doesn't put them on a computer. But I'll get him."

"I'd hate to be on the receiving end of your 'getting'".

"Then you'd better treat her right. Anyway, the field and the cemetery are zoned residential. From what Maddie and I were able to research, the township would have to give up this piece of cemetery land, and pay to have the graves moved."

Logan nodded, and gave his family a silent apology for getting them involved. "Maddie doesn't know you're here, does she?"

"No, not here. She wouldn't tell you, because she wants to save you the pain—because she loves you."

"The feeling's mutual." Logan's mind worked through the possibilities and the effects. He almost didn't hear Dena speak.

"Let them have their development."

That got his attention. "What?"

"I mean this one. You made a mistake, coming here." She pointed to the headstone before them. "Lisette isn't here. You can talk to her anywhere. They want to move some graves? Fine—we'll find a nice plot elsewhere."

"I will not let those bastards disrespect the memory of my family—"

"It's disrespectful to favor the empty vessels of loved ones, when their spirits would want something else."

"How do you know what they'd want?" Logan realized his fists were clenched. He forced them open and counted slowly, then started when Dena touched his arm.

"I know." She looked up at him, her face reflecting sympathy, but also determination. "And you'd know too, if you stopped to consider how they'd feel about this."

Logan looked, again, to the headstone. No, Lisette wasn't in there. What a fool he'd been. "I'll fight them."

"Of course you will. Hit them with the bad publicity first, see what the PR department has to say about that. But if you lose, let them have their little underhanded battle, because you're going to win the war."

"You're right." He patted Dena on the shoulder, then looked around. This was the first time since he'd started coming that he felt truly at peace. "I won't let this distract me."

Leaping to her feet, Dena let out a war whoop that made Logan flinch. "Sorry! It's just that I hoped you'd come to that conclusion, and I know your family would approve. I also think Lisette is very happy you've found someone new."

"And you," Logan told her gently, "would know." Standing, he dug into his pocket, then sorted through the change he came up with. "You want to help?"

"Just call me Mata Hari." She watched him curiously. "It's about time I got back into real life, too. I'm so tired of people like Crapweasel driving the humanity out of everything that's—what?"

When Logan held his hand out to her, fingers holding two pennies, Dena tilted her head and stared. "Um—retainer fee?"

Logan shook his head. "I have a plan, and for it to work I need your help. Remember, you said that for two cents you'd settle down here? Well, if my plan works, Maddie will be settling down—here—and she'll want her friend to come along with her."

With a grin, Dena took the pennies, then shook his hand. "You just bought yourself a co-conspirator."

No matter how much Tremayne complained, he could find nowhere to park around the courthouse square in Albion. He settled for an empty space a block away, next to the old town hall. The Boston lawyer didn't stop grumbling until he and Maddie, trailed by Dena, reached the intersection of the town's only stop light.

"What a beautiful building," Dena said as they crossed the street. The century old courthouse, built of orange masonry with copper roofs turned sea foam green with age, featured arched windows and battlements. A clock tower rose far above the two and three story buildings surrounding it.

"Interesting architecture," Tremayne agreed grudgingly, "but what's inside is what we worry about."

Maddie hid a smile as they sent their briefcases through the security checkpoint. Tremayne had been in a foul mood for the last week, as his legal maneuverings got him little more than a moved up initial hearing. He'd been convinced that these Midwest hicks would be easily pushed around, and she took great pleasure in watching his confidence waver.

As for Maddie, she was completely prepared. Completely. She'd even packed the fifth pair of her favorite brand of pantyhose into her purse, in case of a run, or being tackled, or jumping out of a window, or whatever. Yes, she was prepared. She kept repeating that, like a mantra.

The smallest elevator Maddie had ever seen delivered them to the third floor, where the Circuit court room was adorned with what appeared to be original wood furnishings. As expected, area residents filled the place to overflowing. "The usual suspects," Dena whispered.

Logan, Martin Dunn, and a rather perturbed looking middle aged lawyer in a tweed jacket sat at one of the tables up front. When Maddie took her seat she found herself right across the aisle from Logan, who glanced at her without expression. Behind him sat Judy, Logan's kids, and just about everyone else Maddie had met since coming here, including Lydia, Jake, and a still brooding Tupper.

The crowd hushed when Tremayne stopped by Logan. "I'm looking forward to an opportunity to pay you back for your 'Mexican' coffee."

"Pay me back? Your money's no good here, Gilroy."

Maddie stepped in to prevent a confrontation. "It's not too late to negotiate something a bit less harmful to your client."

On the other side of Logan, Dunn's lawyer leaned forward. "He is *my* client, thank you, even if he does insist Mr. Chandler speak for him, and I should warn you against talking to either of them."

"You're right, Mr. Westerly," Logan told the man. "I'm not a lawyer—I still have a soul." He ignored a wave of laughter from behind him and turned back to Maddie, while Westerly yanked a handkerchief from his pocket and swiped angrily at his glasses. "I believe negotiation times are over. My only suggestion at this point would be that your boss head down to Fort Wayne International, where there are plenty of airplanes already available to take him back to Boston."

"That's right!" Tupper called, while others around him applauded.

A moment later, the bailiff announced the arrival of Judge Randolph Lamar Scott, who quickly waved them back to their seats. As Maddie settled in, she looked over at Logan. She could only imagine how angry he must be at her.

He scribbled something on a piece of paper, then held it up to her. It was a heart.

Someone giggled behind her. Maddie, her heart thudding, tried to pay attention as the judge laid out documents before him, then looked up.

Scott was a slim and mild looking man, with salt and pepper hair. "Now, this is a preliminary hearing, everyone." He looked up over his glasses. "Just as the Plan Commission meeting was preliminary, but there will be no such drama here, understand? I hope none of you think all this will be settled today. Mr. Tremayne."

Tremayne strutted into the open space before the bench. "Your honor, as you can see from the court documents, my client owns land downhill from Mr. Dunn's drive-in theater, and also—more importantly—in the path of drainage from the aforementioned drive-in. As part of the purchasing process, we did routine tests on our property that indicated contamination in the soil and aquifer, which can only have come from Dunn's land."

Logan bolted to his feet. "Routine tests done by whom, Your Honor?" Beside him, Westerly's head almost hit the table.

Judge Scott held up a cautionary hand. "We're getting there, Mr. Chandler. I don't hold on ceremony, but just the same, let's try to keep this from turning into a free-for-all."

Maddie suppressed a sigh. Thank goodness this judge didn't seem too by-the-books, but the other side—as she had trouble calling them—was taking a huge chance letting Logan defend their case. Great kisser he was, attorney he was not.

Tremayne shot Logan a vicious glare. "We're talking about a drive-in, Your Honor, a place where cars parked for half a century. I'm not suggesting Mr. Dunn deliberately dumped hazardous chemicals—but consider five decades of oil leaks, fuel leaks, spills of transmission and brake fluid, radiator fluid—not to mention the original septic system. What about the food? How much popcorn oil, for instance, has soaked into the ground over time?"

Maddie thought about the popcorn Logan knocked from her hand that first night, and for a wild second almost yelled out that there'd been no butter on it.

"We recycle our cooking oil," Dunn began, but Tremayne cut him off.

"Are you saying there has never—*never*—been an accidental spill of oil, or soda fountain syrup, or something from the portable toilets brought in on holiday weekends?"

Dunn's brow furled as he searched his memory, and the longer the silence grew, the worse it looked. With an expression of fake sincerity, Tremayne turned back to the judge.

"Again, I don't suggest it was done deliberately. But there have been many cases of contamination taking place over time. In auto shops, for instance, and dry cleaning establishments. Why not in a fifty year old drive-in? And may I remind Your Honor, waste spills were not nearly as well policed when that business started."

Dena shot Maddie an appealing look, but even if she had been Dunn's attorney, Maddie didn't know what she would say. Tremayne, as much as she hated to admit it, had a point.

"All we're saying is, if there's a chance something is going wrong underground, it needs to be investigated."

Judge Scott leaned forward, staring at Tremayne over his glasses. "And the fact that your company wants to get Mr. Dunn's property has nothing to do with this?"

Good for you, judge, Maddie thought.

"But, Your Honor ..." Tremayne shook his head sadly. "We need a piece of usable land, not a brown zone. Besides, even if Mr. Dunn never sells, my client still owns, or has an option to buy, property on all four sides. If that's being contaminated by our neighbors, we have the right to know."

196

Maddie risked a glance at Logan, and saw him stare at Tremayne with a deep frown. Apparently Logan also saw which way this was heading.

"All right." Scott rubbed his chin for a moment. "I'll allow the suit to go forward, and order more thorough testing of the drive-in property." Then he stared hard at Tremayne. "Testing from an Indiana company chosen by this court, understood?"

Tremayne raised his hands, all innocent. "Of course."

The judge banged his gavel, and the crowd, many of them looking perturbed that nothing more than that had been settled, reluctantly began to break up. Judy reach forward to touch Dunn's hand, and they gave each other a reassuring squeeze. A moment later she also noticed Faith and Conner approach, so she retook her seat to be at their level.

"Are we 'taminated?" Conner asked, while behind him his father and grandmother froze in their tracks.

"Oh, honey, no." Maddie, her throat tightening, gave him a quick hug. "If there's anything at all it's underground, where it can't get you."

"Then why do you have to close the drive-in?" Faith demanded. "Don't you love us?"

Maddie drew back with a gasp, and tried to catch her breath. Before she could speak she felt a shadow over her, and heard Tremayne's voice.

"Maddie has an important job to do, children. She has to make sure bad stuff doesn't go on someone else's land, doesn't she? It's very important work, more important than going to a movie."

Conner, not the least bit convinced, drew himself up and gave Tremayne a hateful glare. "You're a bad man! You just want Marty's drive-in."

Faith nodded. "You're selfish and greedy."

"Oh?" Tremayne looked to Logan, who seemed to be hiding a smile. "I suppose your father told you that?"

Logan shook his head. "My kids are bright enough to know selfish and greedy when they see it, Gilroy."

"Then they're bright enough to know this." Tremayne turned to the children again. "Maddie works for me, children. That means she's working against your father, against Martin Dunn, and against you."

Maddie jerked to her feet and whirled on him. "Gil, you—"

"Do you really want children trusting you, Madison? Like before? Remember what happened before."

Most of the crowd remained in the room, but silence fell over them, silence so total Maddie could hear her own pulse pounding in her temples. After all this time she'd let children depend on her again, and she'd let them down. Her legs buckled, but she felt strong arms around her waist, lowering her to her seat.

"That's enough, Tremayne," Logan warned. "You've used up your chances."

"Then why don't you hit me, Chandler? Right in front of your children and all these witnesses?" Maddie clutched Logan's hands, but he made no motion toward her ex-fiancé. Instead, Tremayne took a taunting step forward.

"There's something else you don't know, children. Because Madison didn't do her job when she first arrived here, we lost money, and to make up for it we got involved in a new development."

Maddie's breath caught.

"To make room for that development, a road has to be built across

198

part of a cemetery. And so, because of Maddie, your mother's grave is going to have to be dug up and moved."

# CHAPTER THIRTEEN

Maddie let go of Logan's hand. "Hit him."

But Logan didn't move at all.

From the back of the room Lydia called, "Knock his block off, Logan. Not a jury in the world will convict you."

"I'll pay the bail," Tupper added.

Finally Logan turned his head, just enough to see his children's confused, wide-eyed expressions.

Tremayne just stood there, with a smug smile that Maddie desperately hoped Logan would wipe off his face. Logan himself, chest heaving, still didn't take action. Instead he looked toward his mother, whose face was as white as Logan's was red.

Judy shook her head. "The children need dinner." Her face a mask, she dragged her protesting grandchildren from the courtroom.

Standing, Maddie drifted into the courtroom's center aisle as she watched them go, and realized she did love those kids. Her eyes narrowed. She turned toward Tremayne.

With great effort, Logan straightened his fingers, then glanced around the room. "You won't get the satisfaction of seeing me in jail,

Tremayne. Not today." He gestured toward his departing family and added, "There'll be another time, especially if your firm plans to follow my family wherever they go."

Tremayne, looking disappointed and relieved at the same time, shook his head. "I'd be happy never to hear your name again."

Maddie swept her hand over the piles of paperwork on Tremayne's table. "How much time did you spend planning to ruin Logan's family to make yourself look good?"

"Don't flatter him—it fell into my lap. I'm well aware of the irony. I find it ... humorous."

"I'm sure you do." Maddie strode forward and, with both arms, swept every briefcase and sheet of paper off the desk. While sheets still fluttered to the floor she whirled around and, with all the strength she could muster, backhanded Tremayne in the face.

While he cartwheeled over the railing behind him she shouted, "How humorous do you find *that?*"

"Maddie!" Logan grabbed her arm, forcing her backward. "That's just what he wanted."

"Sure, but it still felt good."

"But there are witnesses."

The witnesses, as a group, cheered.

"Go, Maddie!"

"Hit him again!"

"Get the other side of his face, make it symmetrical!"

But the commotion died down when Judge Scott threw open the door to his chambers and stormed out. "What the devil's going on out

202

here?"

He stopped in mid stride when Tremayne jolted to his feet and stood there—wobbling a bit—with teeth clenched, eyes flashing, and an angry red mark covering one cheek. "She hit me!" he roared. "In the middle of *your* courtroom!"

Scott, eyes narrowed, turned to Maddie. "Is this true?"

As if it wasn't obvious. Maddie started to say she did, and was proud of it, but then she looked around at the others. Logan, Lydia, Tupper, everyone looked back at her, all innocence, and after a moment Lydia spoke:

"He fell."

Others joined in immediately.

"Tripped right over that railing."

"Terrible thing—"

"We tried to catch him ..."

"Hit his face on a chair."

The judge turned toward Jake, who sat in his wheelchair near the back of the room. "Padre?"

"Everyone stood up," Jake told him, with a placid expression. "Happens to me at ball games all the time."

Scott stared around him for another minute before addressing Tremayne. "I won't tolerate hearsay in my court, counselor. Now all of you get out, I've got a trial this afternoon." He turned, and Maddie caught a glimpse of a smile as he disappeared back into his chambers.

For a long moment Tremayne stood there, hand on his bruise, with a look of disbelief. Maddie realized Tremayne had counted on getting someone thrown into jail for assaulting him almost from the moment he arrived in Indiana, only he'd assumed it would be Logan— and he'd also assumed it would work.

Tremayne turned a murderous gaze on Maddie. "You are *fired*. And the deal is *off*."

"It's not off," Maddie told him, "because the deal was that I wouldn't quit. You just fired me."

Tremayne stared, open mouthed.

"You have it in writing in a hidden file on my computer, and I've got a hard copy," she added.

"We'll take care of Maddie," Logan told him. "I already knew you planned to dig up my family. I won't let you use the dead against the living, and they wouldn't want that, anyway."

It took a moment for Maddie to realize what he meant. She turned to Dena, who sent her a shrug and a blush. A murmur went through the others.

"You knew, eh? Very well." Tremayne gestured to Dena, then pointed at the mess on the floor. "Get these papers together, Hantanawee."

"It's 'Hantaywee'." Dena's voice remained calm, despite the anger flashing in her eyes. She made no attempt to move.

"Really? Well, right now you have a job, whatever your name. Do you want to keep it, or would you like to be blackballed out of the entire field, just as McKinley will be?"

Dena held her pose for a moment more. Then, slowly, she knelt down to begin scooping the papers into a briefcase.

"Dena—" Maddie stepped toward her friend, intending to let her know the people around them would support Dena, just as they would support her, until they could get back on their feet. But Dena held a hand out in a stopping motion.

"I'll stay with the company, Maddie. I'm sorry. I'm not ready to start all over again." She continued working, without looking up.

What? That couldn't be what Maddie had heard. Dena, always willing to speak her mind and live for today, had encouraged her to quit. Now that she'd lost her job, how could Dena stay? Where was the courage her friend always showed? She opened her mouth to argue, but Logan's firm grip on her arm stopped her.

"Let her go," he whispered in her ear. "We each choose our own path. Dena's choice might not be as strange as it seems."

"But—"

"Later. There'll be time to talk to her later."

But Maddie couldn't imagine life ever being the same between her and her former best friend.

Dena finished and climbed to her feet, struggling with two briefcases. Instead of offering to help, Tremayne waved her toward the doorway, then turned to the others. "You wanted personal? I'll give you personal. I'm going to see to it that you spent the rest of your lives in misery. You'll lose your precious drive-in, and I'll pave over your family plot, and by the time I'm done all you'll have to show for it is legal bills, and valueless houses right under the landing path of screaming airliners."

He turned and shoved through the doorway. Dena, loaded down by the briefcases and not looking back, marched right behind him.

"What's this about moving the family plot?" Lydia demanded as soon as the door slammed.

"Later." Logan headed for the door and for a moment, as the crowd filed out, Maddie lost track of him. Everyone wanted to congratulate her, and offer words of encouragement. Then, in the rotunda at the center of the building, she spotted Logan leaning against a railway that looked down two stories, onto the main floor.

He glanced up when she joined him. "You okay?"

Maddie nodded, although she wasn't really sure. She looked down at her legs and realized, with some surprise, that decking Gil hadn't somehow led to a run in her pantyhose. It was a good thing, because she'd never gotten around to having Dena send off for more Sheer Invites.

Logan reached out to wipe a tear from Maddie's cheek. "Lisette had a degree in architecture."

"Oh?" At first she couldn't tell why he'd said it, but then she followed his gaze around the century old courthouse. She'd always thought of buildings by their functions, but this one had an old style beauty, complete with a chandelier, and paintings on the walls. "Oh. I never imagined going to a courthouse for anything but court."

"When it was first built, this wasn't just for the courts: the entire county government was housed here. Anyway, she loved this place. She told me once it spoke to her of optimism, and pride, and the human spirit."

Logan turned to give Maddie his full attention. "I told her it was a shame to waste such a place on lawyers. Sorry about that."

"I'm beginning to see her point."

Frowning, he shook his head. "Blind prejudice against an entire group is never good. And there I was, trying to teach the kids not to do something I was guilty of, myself."

"But with everything he's up to ..." Maddie shuddered, thinking again that she'd been on the same path her ex-fiancé traveled. "I thought you'd be enraged about the cemetery."

"I was enraged, a few days ago. But my outlook ... changed." He reached out to stroke her hair, and she saw something different in his eyes, something brighter—life that hadn't quite been there before. "Come on. I want to show you something."

He led her outside to his van. They left Albion, drove without talking across the county and past Hopewell, and finally stopped in the narrow lane of a cemetery. Maddie had never thought of a cemetery as anything but a place to bury the dead, but as she got out and began taking in the quiet beauty of the place, she could feel some of her tension drain away.

Tree studded hills marked the area, and many of the stones were over a century old. Flowers decorated some gravesites; small flags flew over others.

Logan waited until she'd soaked it in for a moment, then took her hand and led her over quiet paths. "All this fuss brought back those days right after Lise died—that awful grief my family barely got me through. And, 'Grief drives men to serious reflection, sharpens the understanding, and softens the heart'."

"What—was that—?"

"John Adams. I've been doing some research, and it turns out he was a pretty smart guy, if a bit tightly wound. In this case, it was like he was talking right at me, about my time of grief. Reliving that time, and getting smacked around by some of my friends, made me do some serious reflection—and softened my heart. Don't get me wrong, your old flame's still a jerk—"

"I'm sorry about what Gil is doing—"

But Logan stopped her with a finger to her lips, then left the path and led her up a hill. "But that's the point I was making, with Lise and her attitude toward architecture. I always worried that she turned her back on her own dreams when she married me. One day I questioned her about it once too often, and she set me straight.

"She said she'd always love architecture, but she was concerned with the present, and our future. She said places like the courthouse are important, but they're the past."

He stopped, and waved his hand over a small plot near one side of the cemetery. Maddie's heart jumped when she saw the names of the stones before her.

"This is the past, too. Lise isn't here anymore, and neither is my father."

He looked around the cemetery again, then turned back to smile at Maddie. "I think Lise would like it somewhere closer to buildings. If we can't stop this maybe I'll build her a crypt, some place with statues and inscriptions, or an angel on top. I think she'd like that. I also think she wouldn't mind staying where she is. But she wouldn't like me caving in to a bastard like Tremayne, no matter what."

"Would she like you spending that much money?"

"I have money. After going through bankruptcy as a kid, my father turned into a miser." He pulled her into an embrace, and they held each other for a long time. Finally he pulled back, enough to brush his lips against hers. "Mom said she's getting the guest bedroom ready for you."

She gave him a questioning look.

"The law firm paid for your hotel room, yes?"

"Oh." Maddie sank onto the stone bench. She'd burned every bridge behind her, that much was certain. No more paycheck, no more benefits, not even a best friend. "You're a prince. Which is good, because I've become a damsel in distress."

"I can't imagine that."

"You can't? Gil's threats weren't empty. He may not be able to have me disbarred, but he might be able to get me blackballed out of the industry. Even if he can't, there's still the no competition clause in my contract. I can make it for a while on savings … I can sell my furnishings and the Porsche, but— "

"You don't have to sell the Porsche just because it's a little dusty. We've got car washes, you know."

She looked up, and saw him grin at her. "What's on your mind? Do you need full time help in the coffee shop? Does Lydia plan to retire?" As she spoke her heart sank, when she realized Judy would still be at the shop, regardless—any dream of traveling the world with Marty was gone, because Marty's savings would vanish in the fight for his business.

But Logan continued smiling. "If you've learned anything from my family history, it should be that people only stay down if they don't get back up. Or, to put it another way, 'Courage and perseverance have a magical talisman, before which difficulties disappear and obstacles vanish into air'. I figured as a lawyer you'd understand the two dollar words better."

"I've created a monster. How did you memorize all those John Adams quotes so quickly?"

"Crib notes." He sat beside her, lightly rubbing her hand.

"Fine, but here's one for you: 'We have too many high sounding words, and too few actions that correspond with them'."

Logan pursed his lips and stared off into space. "I didn't come across that one—"

"Abigail Adams, John's wife."

"Ah. How do you like that? Lawyers can be successful and still have a personal life." Logan embraced her again, and Maddie thought nothing could be as wonderful as the warmth of his cheek against hers. "It wasn't just words, for my family. We lost our place in Boston, so we just picked ourselves up and started again in Indiana. I find it ironic—" He thought about it, and his smile widened. "I find it *coincidental* that you can now do the same thing. Assuming, that is, you still want to stay in Indiana."

She caught his meaning, and the pleading look in his eyes. Was it only a few weeks ago that she desperately wanted to get back to Boston? What awaited her there now? No job. No family. Certainly there was no pull to return to her townhouse, which never felt like home even when Dena lived there.

"But I still want to practice law," she heard herself murmur, as she drew away and glanced off across the cemetery.

Logan cupped her chin, and gently brought her attention back to him. "For what purpose?"

"To make a difference. To defend what's right. To bring justice to people like Marty Dunn. To do the opposite of all the things I did before."

"Then here's the perfect place for you." He kissed the tip of her nose. "Tremayne might find he has less influence over Indiana's legal community than he thinks, and a non-competition clause only counts if you're competing with him. Right?"

She nodded, but it wasn't Tremayne she thought about. Logan's optimism still shone like a light against all the darkness she'd encountered lately, and she couldn't help being swept up in it. "I'll think it over." If she couldn't be a lawyer she'd find some other way to help people, no matter where she ended up.

"You'll be the lawyer," Logan told her, as if reading her mind, "And I'll keep you stocked in coffee, and rub your back after a long day in court. It'll all work out."

"You do a lot more than serve coffee." As she said it, she caught the double meaning, and could tell by his grin that he did, too.

"Whatever you wish." Logan stood, pulled Maddie to her feet, and led her toward the parked van. "Meanwhile, since Crapweasel abandoned you, I'll give you a ride back to Hopewell."

But almost as soon as he started the van, an alarming flapping noise emerged from under the hood, and red lights lit up on the vehicle's instrument panel. Logan hurriedly shut the engine off, then climbed out to look under the hood. "Well, isn't that something—my van dies in a cemetery."

"At least you're using your imagination." She got out and watched as he examined the engine compartment. "Most guys claim they've just run out of gas." Maddie wasn't overly concerned, until she realized there was no sign of another living person. As lovely as the cemetery looked in the daylight, she didn't relish the idea of testing her imagination with an overnight stay.

He shot her a wry smile, then turned back to his examination. "Here's the problem—broken belt. Did you bring your cell phone?"

Maddie's hand automatically went to her purse, but then dropped to her side. "I left it in Crapweasel's car. They're not appreciated in courtrooms."

"Right, which is why mine's at the shop. Well, then, can I borrow your pantyhose?"

Maddie stared at him. "Are you serious?"

"On occasion. It's an old trick I saw my dad use many years ago— pantyhose can be kind of wound up and tied together to make a

211

temporary belt. It should hold to get us to the shop, but ..." He bent over the engine compartment, frowning. "Engine designs have changed, and this one's a lot longer. I don't suppose you have a spare?"

"Two pair?" No way could this be happening.

Logan shrugged, and turned back to puttering with the engine. "A lot to ask, I know. Besides, it's not that much of a walk to the nearest house."

"In these shoes it is." Maddie felt like her last pair of Sheer Invites were shouting from inside her purse. Just in case, she'd brought them. Just in case. Coincidence? But they didn't sell her brand around here, and now that she was jobless, luxury items from the East Coast was over of her budget.

Oh, for Heaven's sake. What was so important about some heavy-duty hosiery from Boston, made for stale old ladies who wanted to protect themselves from life? What was wrong with Indiana products? Or bare legs, for that matter? Pantyhose were out of style, anyway.

Reaching into her purse, she pulled out her last pair of Sheer Invites and shook the bag. Logan turned, took the sight in, and arched an eyebrow. "Were you a Boy Scout?"

"No. This is just what coincidence is."

Laughing, Logan took her in his arms. "Do I get to take the other pair off?"

"Not this time." She kissed him, but then shoved him away. "Not in a cemetery in the middle of the day, anyway. Maybe I'll invest in a nice pair of lacy thigh-highs for next time."

His look held such raw lust that she almost changed her mind. "At least you're giving me something to look forward to. All right—let's take care of the immediate problem, then go plot some strategy. Seeing as how you had a contract with the opposition, you can't bill me for this, you know."

"Oh, so that's why you're so anxious to get my help," she teased. "All right—a little pro bono work never hurt anyone. 'Let justice be done, though the heavens should fall.'" But that didn't solve their problems ... not by a long shot.

Logan grinned. "Or, as Adams would say if he were around today, let's go put Crapweasel in his place."

# CHAPTER FOURTEEN

Gilroy Tremayne, for all his faults, was not the kind of man to be beaten easily.

Or maybe that *was* one of his faults, Maddie thought, as she took her seat behind Logan in the Circuit Court Room. She looked over at the still empty table on the other side of the aisle, and wondered what kind of unpleasant surprises her ex-fiancé would have, now that the soil test results were back. Everyone had spent a tense three weeks waiting for the next court date.

Martin Dunn turned to give her a reassuring wink. "Don't worry, Maddie. My family has always taken very good care of our business—after all, we lived right next door." Beside him, Logan nodded encouragement.

But Maddie wasn't reassured. If Tremayne couldn't dig up something legitimate, he'd find a way to invent a problem, especially with it now so personal. Meanwhile she was stuck behind the railing, with no way to help in the defense of the drive-in—at least, no way that wouldn't violate the no-competition agreement with her former employer. She'd helped Westerly with legal advice as the other lawyer prepared his case, but until the test results came back there was no way to know what they would have to defend against next.

Beside her, Judy patted her on the arm. "I'm glad to have you with us, dear."

"I wouldn't have missed it." She was glad too, but felt like she'd been cut adrift. Her townhouse was on the market, and all she owned in storage, although Logan claimed to have room for everything at his home.

*Their* home, he'd insisted, but she remained resistant to the idea of depending on his kindness. All her life, she'd refused to depend on anyone but herself, and until the death of Dena's fiancé she'd refused to let anyone else depend on her.

Maddie sighed, and shifted on the hard wooden bench. She missed Dena, who—on orders from Tremayne, Maddie desperately hoped— had made no contact with her since the last time they'd been together, in this same courtroom.

But she'd been comforted by the love of a good family, who treated her as one of their own. Maddie looked down to her left, past Judy, where Faith and Conner waited more or less patiently. Beyond them sat Lydia, Tupper, everyone—the same full house as last time. All her new friends and family. Now, at least, she fought on the right side. Win or lose.

The main door opened, and Gilroy Tremayne strode in like a general on the battlefield. Behind him, Dena lugged only one briefcase, and with a shock Maddie realized her other hand clutched a copy of the thick John Adams biography. What was this? A gift from Adam Quincy, for being loyal to the company?

After Dena came another, much greater shock. A new player, carrying his own briefcase, stomped in: A stout man with white, thinning hair and a gray, custom tailored suit. His gaze immediately went to Logan's table, then behind it to Maddie.

Their stares locked. Maddie almost stood from pure habit, but her legs probably wouldn't have held her up as she watched the most senior of senior partners sweep past her. Adam Quincy looked exceedingly displeased to be here.

Beside Logan, Westerly darted a look toward his competition and started to shake. He must have heard of Quincy, but hadn't expected to see the man himself walk through the door.

Dena didn't look toward her, but even though seeing her friend ignore her felt like a punch in the stomach, Maddie concentrated on matters at hand. What did Quincy's appearance mean? Clearly the matter was a big deal to Quincy, Dixon and Tremayne, to bring not only Gil—the nephew of a senior partner—but also the main boss himself.

Before she had time to think on it more, the door to the judge's chambers opened, and Randolph Lamar Scott made his way to the bench carrying a manila envelope. When everyone took their seats, he glared around at the packed room.

"I don't want to see a repeat of the last performance, whether I'm in the room or not."

Tremayne impulsively rubbed the side of his face, and Maddie caught herself massaging a hand she'd thought broken.

"The records will show that I hold here the test results on the High View Drive-In, still sealed, and that I am breaking the seal at this time."

An unnecessary precaution, but perhaps the judge was trying to head off any charges of tampering. The crowd stilled, and everyone held their breath as Scott rifled through a stack of papers. But minutes passed, and, although no one dared speak, the audience squirmed in their uncomfortable seats. As Maddie had learned during her research, Scott held a reputation as a meticulous man.

Finally the judge looked up, one eyebrow raised, and handed

copies of the report to his bailiff. She, in turn, passed them to the two attorney's tables, and the crowd sat through another agonizing silence.

Maddie could immediately tell something was wrong. Logan's shoulders sagged, and Dunn's eyes widened as he took in the details.

On the other side, Maddie noticed, Quincy studied the report with pursed lips, while Tremayne hardly glanced at it. Strange ... Gil also had a reputation as a stickler, and this report was pivotal to his case. She was still studying her former boyfriend when she noticed a commotion in front of her.

"This is impossible," Dunn gasped, while Logan tried to calm him. "I tell you, I take care of my place!" His skin was pasty, and his eyes bulging.

"Don't jump to conclusions," Logan told him in a low voice.

"But these *are* the conclusions!" Dunn shook his head violently. "How can it be? What did I do?" His breath became labored, and Maddie feared he would hyperventilate.

"Marty, please." Judy jumped to her feet, and leaned forward to grab Dunn's shoulders. "Calm down."

"Order," Judge Scott said, but he barely tapped his gavel.

Tremayne, looking so smug he could burst, hooked a thumb toward the other table. "Your Honor, this is most unbecoming."

Westerly shot the other lawyer a hateful glare. "Your Honor, we request a short recess."

Scott nodded. "Ten minutes, counselor. Take Mr. Dunn out for some air."

Logan and Westerly led Dunn out, and when Judy got up Maddie decided to join them. Tremayne started to protest, but she shot him a glare meant to communicate everything she felt right now, and he clamped his mouth shut.

In the hallway outside, Dunn fell into a chair while Judy knelt beside it, trying to comfort him with little success. Maddie squeezed his shoulder, then turned to where Logan and Westerly, heads together, continued to study the test results. "How bad is it?"

Logan glanced up, then gave her a second look, his eyes showing his gratitude for her presence. "As bad as it can get. Major contamination of the subsurface soil, with signs that it's spread onto neighboring properties. Nothing seems to have gotten into the water table yet, but this shows hydrocarbons, phosphates, acids—just about anything that might ever be generated at a place like the drive-in."

Maddie poured over the numbers, and although not an expert in this area, she could tell it was bad. "How can this be? I could understand if it was deliberate dumping, but I can't believe a man like Marty wouldn't be careful."

Logan shook his head, looking mystified. "Someone in the past, even illegal dumping by trespassers, maybe in winter when he didn't watch as carefully ... it doesn't seem likely, but what other explanation is there?"

"Contamination by lawyer," Maddie suggested, remembering the look on Tremayne's face that she'd wanted so badly to slap off. Again.

But again Logan shook his head. "How? An independent testing company, and sealed results ...?"

The courtroom door opened. Tremayne stepped through, followed closely by Quincy and Dena, and this time Maddie's friends didn't have it in them to make threats or insults.

Dena, who'd left the briefcase behind but still clutched the book, hovered on the edge of the group along with Quincy. Tremayne ignored Maddie and stepped in front of the still pale and shaken Dunn, who looked up with the expression of a beaten man.

"I'm sorry, Mr. Dunn." Tremayne seemed sincere. Of course, Tremayne was an accomplished liar. "This isn't what we wanted."

"Oh?" Logan clearly didn't believe it for a second. "The drive-in shut down? That's not what you wanted?"

"Shut down, yes," Tremayne replied smoothly. "Contaminated, no. Judging from these numbers, a huge amount of soil is going to have to be dug up and taken to a hazardous waste landfill, and replaced with new soil. The cost will be tremendous, and now that it's in the open, the present owner must bear that cost."

Dunn jolted as if struck. Beside him, a tear rolled down Judy's cheek.

"I guess we're all losers, then," Maddie said, although she knew Tremayne planned something that would bring him out on top.

In that, she wasn't disappointed. "Not necessarily. The truth is, we still need your land for the airport. Based on our preliminary reports we already believed there was gross contamination, so the development company has agreed to a plan that may be beneficial to all of us."

He paused, and while everyone else chewed on that Maddie looked at Quincy. The senior partner studied Tremayne closely, and Maddie realized he knew little more about Tremayne's plotting than she did. She almost blurted it out when she realized that, just as her ex came to judge her, Quincy was here to observe Tremayne's work. That must be galling, she thought with satisfaction.

"What plan?" Logan demanded.

"The developer will take Mr. Dunn's land and pay for the clean-up. It's as simple as that: We get our airport, Martin Dunn gets out from underneath not only the cost of cleaning a brown zone, but also the possibility of fines and criminal prosecution." He leaned down a bit to add, as if talking to a child, "We believe it wasn't on purpose, Martin, but a federal prosecutor might not."

After a moment Westerly ventured, "How much will you offer for the land?"

Tremayne looked surprised. "Offer? Nothing, of course. By signing the property over to us Mr. Dunn will break even—no profit, but also no loss. Preferable to bankruptcy, or years spent in a minimum security federal prison—don't you agree, Mr. Dunn?"

Logan looked to Maddie, who shrugged. She could tell he seethed as much as she did, but they followed the leads of the others, who silently waited on Dunn. The old man, defeat evident in his posture, stared at the floor a for long moment then straightened with great effort. "What else is there?"

Maddie looked around, searching for something—anything. Like Dunn, Judy and Logan looked devastated. Tremayne kept his facade of comforting helper, while Dena and Westerly pasted on their professional neutral faces. Quincy continued to watch Tremayne, his eyes narrowed.

"Well, then." With a mild smile, Tremayne gestured grandly toward the courtroom. "Shall we go speak to the judge? Perhaps we can clear this up with some simple paperwork. And, since Mr. Dunn will no longer have any ownership in the disputed area, the zoning issue will become a moot point."

Dunn laid a hand on Judy's arm, with an apologetic look, then turned to lead everyone back toward the courtroom. Maddie fell in beside Logan and saw not anger on his face, but sadness. It wasn't just a gathering place he was losing, but a part of his past, and the chance for his mother's future happiness. She wondered if even a family as strong as this one could recover from such a blow, and whether it would sabotage her future with them before it could begin.

Tremayne started to take up the rear, but Dena let him by, and Maddie glimpsed him lightly brush his assistant as he passed.

It all happened very quickly then.

"Stop!" Dena screamed, and Maddie whirled around in time to see her friend swing the thick, hardback book as hard as she could—right into Tremayne's face. Tremayne stumbled backward into the chair and sent it, and him, crashing to the ground. He lay there, clutching his nose, while Dena slammed the book down with such force that a boom echoed through the courthouse. She pointed an accusing finger at him.

"He groped me! Again! He's been doing it for weeks! You lousy—" She aimed a kick at the fallen man's groin, but Logan dragged her backward before it could connect.

"You *groped* your assistant?" Logan demanded in a disbelieving voice. He turned on Quincy, who shoved past Westerly with a scowl. "Is this something all you Boston lawyers do?"

"We most certainly do not!"

Maddie had to agree. The code of conduct at Quincy, Dixon and Tremayne was very clear, and for all Tremayne's faults, it shocked her that he would do something like this. But Dena struggled to free herself from Logan's grip, calling Tremayne names Maddie couldn't believe she knew.

"He's made passes at me since before he fired Maddie! He kept trying to corner me in his office—wanted to show his appreciation, the sexist son of a—"

"I didn't!" Tremayne scrambled to his feet, still holding his nose with one hand. His voice now sounded like a cartoon character. "I would never—Maddie, tell them!"

Dena looked to Maddie, and Maddie caught a gleam in the other woman's eye. Something was up, and Maddie couldn't imagine why she shouldn't play along. "Well, when we both worked at the law firm he did try to get me into bed."

"But we were engaged!"

"That doesn't mean you couldn't respect my wishes. I had a very strict upbringing." There was definitely more to this than met the eye, but despite herself Maddie was beginning to enjoy seeing Tremayne squirm.

"Just a moment." Quincy glanced behind him, and saw a gap in the courtroom's double doors filled solidly with faces. "This is a very serious allegation, and not one that should be played out in such a public setting."

"Yeah?" Dena's voice didn't lower one decibel. "Well, it wouldn't have started if he hadn't tried to play in a *private* setting."

Quincy held up a restraining hand, but turned a hard stare on Tremayne. "I'm only saying, let's complete the business at hand, then deal with this——situation."

"You deal with this situation." Dena tore herself away from Logan's grasp. "Because I quit." She swept past Tremayne, who flinched, then disappeared into the rotunda.

"What just happened?" Westerly asked, after a confused silence.

"I'd say," Logan told him, "Marty's not the only person Crapweasel tried to mess around with." He scooped up the book, which made Tremayne flinch again, then took Maddie's arm and marched into the courtroom.

The crowd scrambled back to their seats, and pretended they'd been sitting there patiently the whole time. "Who's Crapweasel?" Westerly demanded, but he had to hustle to follow everyone else inside, and didn't get his answer.

As if he'd been waiting, Judge Scott entered as soon as everyone was in place. He glanced at Tremayne, who now held a handkerchief to his nose, and took in the empty chair beside the injured lawyer. "I must say, Mr. Quincy, some of the activities involving your law firm call your reputation into question."

Now it was Quincy's turn to look as if he'd been hit. He squared his shoulders. "I assure you, Your Honor, there will be some house cleaning in my organization."

Tremayne, whose nose was beginning to resemble that of a circus clown, turned toward him with a "who, me?" look.

"Very well. You've read the report; do you have any comments?"

Tremayne nodded, then winced in pain. "I bewieve we've reached a congwusion—"

The audience tittered, while Quincy caught Judge Scott's attention. "My apologies, Your Honor. I think you'll find—"

"Just a moment, Your Honor." Logan held up one hand. With the other, he held a single sheet of paper, sporting Quincy, Dixon and Tremayne letterhead, covered with scratches that Maddie recognized as Tremayne's handwriting. "I have—ah—just a moment." He studied the paper. Westerly and Dunn looked over his shoulder, blocking Maddie's view. Now what?

Scott waited patiently, until Logan turned from the paper and caught Westerly's look. Both men nodded, and Logan pushed his chair back. "Your Honor, I'd like to enter this into evidence." He stepped toward the bench, waving the paper, but a bailiff rushed forward to block him.

Scott raised an eyebrow, but it was Tremayne's reaction that caught Maddie's attention. As soon as he caught sight of the paper, the attorney gasped. Blood drained from his face—except the little trickle from his nose—and he also shoved his chair back. "*Objection!*"

He dashed toward Logan, grabbing for the paper, but Logan merely turned and placed one finger, lightly, against the tip of Tremayne's nose. The other man, with a squeak of agony, fell back long enough for Logan to place the paper in the bailiff's hands. By the time Tremayne could see again, Scott was already looking it over.

"So. It seems, Mr. Tremayne, that you've done some very careful research. You knew there are only a few environmental testing companies doing this kind of work in this area. I see here a flow chart leading from each of those companies to a variety of people— managers, contractors, cousins, mistresses—all showing a more or less direct connection from each testing company to either the development company you represent, or your own law firm."

Scott looked up, giving Tremayne a cold stare. "Quite a six degrees of separation type of thing, wouldn't you say?"

"I—I don't—they—how did he get that paper?"

Scott turned to Logan, who shrugged. "I found it on the floor next to our table just now. At first I thought it was something we dropped. It must have fallen out of Tremayne's briefcase during our little ... disturbance outside."

The briefcase did, indeed, stand open, but Maddie couldn't imagine Tremayne would chance bringing such an incriminating document into the courtroom. She looked around, studying each face, until she realized two people who'd been there before had vanished. Dena—and Tupper.

Tupper, who wore his emotions on his sleeve. Tupper, who'd have to leave so the guilt didn't show on his face. Tupper, who was no doubt exchanging high fives with Dena right this moment.

Tupper and Dena. Her friends.

Maddie sat back, her throat tight, and tried to look innocent herself.

"Well." Scott's face flushed, and he frowned deeply as he looked over the paper again. Maddie realized he was trying hard to reign in his temper, but finally the judge leaned forward. "Clearly, an investigation into the possibility of bribery, or blackmail, or something equally heinous, is in order. I'll make contact with the proper authorities."

"We will cooperate completely, Your Honor." Quincy glanced at Tremayne, who slunk back to his seat. "I believe the investigators will find we've cleaned up the debris in our law firm."

Tremayne, for once, was speechless.

"Very well. Until they turn in their reports, it's clear a postponement—"

"Just a moment, Your Honor." Maddie shot to her feet, as a plan formed in her mind. So the contamination report was faked, which meant Dunn could continue to operate his drive-in. The problem was, Dunn didn't want to. That left it up to her to take care of other business. "I'd like to call one witness to the stand."

Westerly moaned, and dropped his head into his hands.

Still clutching his nose with one hand, Tremayne waved wildly with the other. "She hab a no competition claubs!"

"Shut up!" Quincy barked, before turning an embarrassed look to Scott. "Excuse me, Your Honor. I know it's not appropriate, but if I could have just a moment with Miss McKinley?"

Scott threw up his hands. "For all intents and purposes, you're on your own time, now."

Quincy turned to Maddie. "Madison, please."

She met him in the aisle, but it was clear from the craned necks and the blanket of silence that they would not be speaking privately. Quincy hesitated for a moment, glancing around, but then forged on. "Under the circumstances, I believe we'd be willing to release you from the terms of your contract."

"They're trying to weasel out of getting sued," Logan translated.

"Please." Shaking his head, Quincy gave Maddie his full attention. "Madison—you must believe that as senior partner I wouldn't condone this kind of practice."

"Oh, come on. Since the moment I joined the firm, you've made it clear anything goes."

"Is that what you thought?"

"It's what I saw. It's how the associates get to be junior partners, by winning their cases and bringing cash into the firm. If you didn't encourage it, surely you saw it."

Quincy half turned, his shoulders slumping, and Maddie saw something different about the man who once intimidated her so. He was suddenly not a high powered lawyer, but an old man with thinning hair and creases across his face. He took a deep breath, and looked back at her. "Do you know why I brought you into the firm?"

"You said I had the hunger."

"Yes. The hunger for justice, for the rule of law. The same reason I came on board, so long ago . . ." He shook his head. "I saw John Adams in you, but I lost that vision in myself. As Adams said, 'Old minds are like old horses; you must exercise them if you wish to keep them in working order.' Maybe I stopped exercising my mind. I became too interested in our status and our profit, and I forgot why we're supposed to be here."

He shot a glance at Tremayne, his eyes glittering. "I'm going to

227

clean house. Yes, indeed. We're going to work for justice again, not dodge it. And I'd like to start by offering you a soon to be vacated position as a partner. You could help turn us around."

A partner. Not only a partner, but a partner in a firm dedicated to law, instead of profit. A chance to make a real difference, to fight for justice, to right wrongs, just as she'd dreamed of doing in law school.

Logan still stood before the bench, perfectly still, a smile glued to his face. "That's great, Maddie." He took a breath and added, "You broke the glass ceiling." Here and there a few people nodded, their smiles just as fake. Others looked back and forth at each other, with dismayed expressions.

So here it was, what Maddie had always worked for. But it wasn't, of course. She'd been looking for—what? Absolution? Forgiveness for her sister's death, all those years ago?

Logan stared at her, holding his breath.

Her sister's death wasn't her fault. She didn't have to work toward some kind of redemption, but she still wanted to help people. How much help to individuals would she be, working eighty hour weeks in a Boston office building?

How could she ever leave behind that man, and his two marvelous children? She didn't have to—she could have it all. Fulfillment in a career, and love, and a family. All it took was faith. Belief in something she couldn't see or touch.

She smiled at her former boss, grateful for the chance he took on her so long ago, but shook her head. "'If we do not lay ourselves in the service of mankind, whom should we serve?'"

Many of the onlookers murmured in confusion, but Quincy just smiled. "Adams would be very proud of you. As for me, I'm sorry to lose such a valuable employee, but my loss is Indiana's gain. Before these witnesses, you're released from your contract."

Logan let a long breath out, and slumped against the bench.

"Thank you, Mr. Quincy." *Now, on to business.* Maddie moved past the railing, and waved Logan aside. "I don't believe the conditions of my contract will count here, but I really do need to call one witness."

"Witness?" Judge Scott looked perplexed. "We're far from that point, Ms. McKinley."

"Please, indulge me. I'd like to call Martin Dunn."

Dunn looked astonished, but hurried to the witness stand when Scott gestured him forward. The bailiff swore him in, and everyone turned expectantly to Maddie—who knew what she wanted to do, but still wasn't entirely sure how to go about it.

"Mr. Dunn ... do you like running the drive-in?"

"Well, of course—"

"May I remind you that you placed your hand on a Bible, and you're under oath?"

Dunn closed his mouth.

"Marty ..." Her voice softening, Maddie stopped by the stand. "Do you really want to continue running the drive-in?"

With a glance out at the audience, Dunn sighed. "No. No, I don't."

A gasp rose from everyone in the room. Logan looked as if he'd just been slammed by the book he still held, but Maddie just nodded. "Then why do you continue?"

"Because ... oh, you know why, Maddie. None of my family wants to take over, and every perspective buyer wants to tear the place down. I just can't stand to disappoint everyone like that."

"I understand. But what if someone was willing to take over the operation of the drive-in? Someone who would never mention it, until they realized you not only deserved a rest, but wanted one?"

Maddie turned, and saw understanding begin to dawn on Logan's face. "Someone who might even want to expand the operation. Say, a coffee shop in the daytime, and during winter?"

Dunn rubbed his chin. "A combination coffee shop and drive-in theater?"

"Where would the world be without innovation?" Maddie turned again to Logan, all too aware she'd never discussed the idea with him.

"Coincidentally—" Logan flashed a grin at Maddie "—I've been thinking about expanding my own operations. Lydia could become a branch manager, and Tupper could work for me full time. And the kids could help, of course. Faith? Conner? Do you approve of the idea?"

"Yeah!" The whole bench shuddered as the kids jumped up and down.

"The drive-in would go on," Maddie concluded. "What do you think of that idea, Mr. Dunn?"

"I think—" Dunn paused to clear his throat. "I think it suits me right down to the ground."

Maddie turned to the judge, but had to wait for the cheering to settle down before she could speak. Scott made no attempt to quiet the crowd. "No further questions, Your Honor."

Scott turned a questioning look to Quincy, who raised a dismissive hand. "No questions at this time, Your Honor. Although it occurs to me such a business might be a nice anchor for a shopping district, or a public gathering point for a residential subdivision."

Scott nodded. "You may step down, Mr. Dunn."

"Wait!" Logan called. "I have something, while Mr. Dunn is still under oath." He dashed forward to take Dunn's arm. Onlookers gasped when he waved Westerly aside, dropped the book on their table, then shoved the table out of the way to leave only the rail between him and where Judy sat. "Maddie, would you please sit beside my mother?"

Maddie did so, with a glance at Scott, but the judge threw up his hands. "What makes you think I'm in charge?"

Logan sent Scott a smile of thanks, before turning back to Dunn. "The community's taken care of, Marty. It's time to think about what's most important to you." At Dunn's questioning look, Logan reached into his pocket, and produced a small jewelry store box. "I believe you've got one of these in your pocket? And I'll remind you, you're still under oath."

Dunn's face reddened. "How did you—?"

"You kept taking it out and looking at it, at work. Tupper saw you. Now's the time, Marty."

Beside her, Maddie heard Judy gasp. Maddie practically jumped in her chair, overjoyed at what she knew Logan was leading to. And since he'd carried a ring box in his own pocket, Logan must have planned all along to put Dunn on the spot.

When Dunn still hesitated, Logan smiled and led him to the rail. "It's really easy, Marty. I'll show you. Take the box out of your pocket."

Hands shaking, Marty withdrew a box that looked remarkably like the one Logan held.

"Good. Now you kneel, like this." Making sure Dunn followed his actions, Logan knelt on one knee.

Right in front of Maddie.

She froze, afraid to breathe, wondering if this could be part of the

231

demonstration. Logan, his lips turned up in a sly smile, looked to Dunn instead of her. "Now, you need to use the correct name, but otherwise it goes like this."

His head turned, gaze boring into Maddie's, and she felt her heart jump. "Madison ..."

"Judy ..." Dunn gulped.

"I never thought I'd get a second chance like this."

"I never thought I'd find a woman who could make me this happy again."

Without taking his eyes from Maddie, Logan hissed an aside: "Very good, keep it up."

Logan's ring box looked very ... real. "Where did you get—?"

"Jewelry store next door. Fixed my watch, remember? Great guy, always up for a rush order, which I'm making use of right now."

"Logan ..." It *was* real.

"Please, I'm showing my friend Marty how to make all our dreams come true." Logan reached over the rail to take Maddie's hand, and out of the corner of her eye she saw Dunn do the same with Judy. "Maddie, I got so tied up with work, and activism, and getting through life, I forgot about living it."

"Judy, I was so worried about the concerns of everyone else, I never got around to taking care of my needs."

Red faced, Judy fanned herself with her other hand.

As one, the two men snapped open the small cases and held out two uncannily similar diamond rings. "I'm ready to live life again, Maddie. I want to live it with you."

"I need you, Judy. I need you to be with me."

Maddie put her free hand over her mouth, willing herself not to cry, and to stop shaking.

"Success is not about business, Maddie. It's not about fighting an airport, or the perfect blend of coffee, or a comfortable income. It's about happiness." He slipped the ring onto her finger. "Marry me. Make me the most successful man on earth."

"Judy, I've always wanted to see the world, but now I realize it would be an empty, useless trip without you. What I really wanted was right there, all along. You. Come travel the world with me, as my wife." Maddie could only assume Judy now wore a ring—her complete attention was elsewhere.

She felt a tear trickle down her cheek, but she also had to laugh when she realized Logan was pale as a legal document. He stared up at her, eyes hopeful, waiting.

Well, how could there be any doubt? She reached across the rail and into his arms, and as she spoke, she heard the same word come from Judy:

"Yes!"

Judge Scott's gavel pounded down. "I sentence the four of you to life."

# Epilogue

Maddie smiled when the van door opened and Logan, wearing his newly designed "High View Drive-In and Coffee Shop" T-shirt, climbed into the driver's seat. "Major crisis averted?"

"Just a small equipment snafu, the kind Tupper will be able to handle on his own once he gets some experience." He leaned over to kiss her, then drew back with a bemused smile. "You were right about his girlfriend: she's great with the concession customers. The spiked pink hair takes a little getting used to, though."

"My theory was, anyone who can operate an all-night towing service can run a snack counter. Oh, and I was thinking orange for myself, maybe a Mohawk style." She scooted over, so she could snuggle against his shoulder. "Alone at last."

"Yep." Logan kissed the top of her head. "Mom's packing for her honeymoon, the kids are on the playground, and I'm here with my still blonde fiancé, planning our wedding."

"Is that what we're doing? I thought we came to watch a comedy about people from different worlds who fall in love."

"Babe, we lived that story." They held each other in silence for a moment, while the sun touched the edge of the horizon and Logan ran his hand up and down Maddie's arm, making her shiver. "Are you

235

getting cold? Would you like some coffee?"

"What flavor?"

As if she'd said yes, he pulled the thermos out and filled a cup. "I tasted it already. Trust me."

"Yeah, right." She sipped, and let the taste slide over her tongue. "This is ..."

Logan waited, with a worried expression.

"This is wonderful. I can't believe it—is it apple I'm tasting?"

"Red Delicious. I got the idea from our first evening together, when you ate the apple."

"Put it on the menu." She leaned back into his arms, taking slow sips to extend the moment.

"Summer will be over soon," Logan said shortly, "and so will busy season. Have you given any more thought to the consulting job they offered you?"

"To work for the same development company you fought so long? Wouldn't that be a bit too ironic even for us?"

"It would be a great way to start your new law firm. They do still own a lot of land around here, and you might be able to guide them toward some more community friendly uses for it."

"Hmmmm ..." Now that she'd been released from her contract with Quincy, Dixon and Tremayne—which treated her and Dena with kid gloves, as long as they didn't register formal complaints over ex-partner Gilroy Tremayne—she was free to pursue a law career in Indiana. It helped that in addition to verbally abusing Dena, Tremayne really had made a pass at her—having decided she should be beneath him in more ways than one. Maddie had to admire Dena's restraint in doing nothing more than secretly record his actions. "Dena and I talked, and we're leaning toward specializing in assistance to small businesses."

"Not much money in that."

"No, but a lot of satisfaction." She twisted around to look at him. "Speaking of satisfaction, I think I should keep my work load light, just in case you want to use some of that down time over the winter to produce a little personal dividend."

He gazed into her eyes, as his smile widened. "I see a lot of profit in that idea."

"What can I say? I love kids."

"But how do you really feel about giving up the corner office in a high powered law firm?"

"As John Adams said—"

"I thought he'd pop up in the conversation."

"—He said, 'as much as I converse with sages and heroes, I long for rural and domestic scene, for the warbling of birds and the prattling of my children'."

"Prattling children, I like that. Clearly, if we have a son, we should name him John."

"Still ... wouldn't my involvement in that sort of work be quite a coincidence?"

"Baby making?"

"Helping small businesses. What with you being one, at least until your chain of drive-in coffee shops takes off."

"Oh?" He pressed his lips against her forehead. "So you believe in coincidence, now? First I'd better tell you what Tupper just confessed to me."

"What?"

"He didn't wreck Mallie's tow truck. When he found out why you were here he was mad at first, but when he saw how upset the kids were, he realized you must be a good person. So he repainted the side of the truck with an encouraging little message, then followed me around until he found a chance to—coincidentally—drive by and give me a sign."

"Really?" Maddie grinned. "Who would have known he had it in him? I didn't plan to tell you this, but now ..."

"Now what?"

"It wasn't coincidence that Tupper worked both for the drive-in and for the law firm. During our last conversation, Quincy admitted he encouraged Tupper to take the job at the drive-in, in the hopes of getting a spy on the other side."

With a startled laugh, Logan shook his head. "Okay, so maybe not all of life is a coincidence. But you did open the door to my van."

"And you did jump me ..."

"Something I plan to make a regular habit. Then you went looking for a good cup of coffee, and I just happened to own a coffee shop."

"Which just happened to have an office space for rent above it."

The coming attractions began, and Logan watched Maddie in the silver screen's flickering light. "Which brought you to me, just when I needed you most. Coincidence?"

"No." She leaned forward to kiss him again. "Fate."

# About the Author

Mark R. Hunter is the author of three other romantic comedies: *Radio Red*, *Storm Chaser*, and its sequel, *The Notorious Ian Grant*, as well as a related story collection, *Storm Chaser Shorts*. He also published a young adult adventure, *The No-Campfire Girls*, and a humor collection, *Slightly Off the Mark*.

In addition, Mark collaborated with his wife, Emily, on the history books *Hoosier Hysterical: How the West Became the Midwest Without Moving At All*; *Images of America: Albion and Noble County*; and *Smoky Days and Sleepless Nights: A Century or So With The Albion Fire Department.*. His short works appeared in the anthologies *My Funny Valentine, Strange Portals: Ink Slingers' Fantasy/Horror Anthology*, and *The Legend of Ol' Man Wickleberry (and His Demise)*.

Mark is a 911 dispatcher and volunteer firefighter in rural Indiana, where he lives with Emily and their dog, Beowulf. He's online at www.markrhunter.com, blogs at https://markrhunter.blogspot.com/, and can be found hanging out on Facebook at https://www.facebook.com/MarkRHunter/ and Twitter as @MarkRHunter.

Made in United States
North Haven, CT
28 May 2024

53032166R00135